CLARA WU

AND THE

JADE LABYRINTH

BY VINCENT YEE

DEDICATION

Dedicated to all the Asian Americans who were affected by the pandemic.

In memory of Andrew

CHAPTERS

ONE

The black-inked-soaked bristles glided along the page, and the brush swiftly lifted away. Soon, fiery embers emanated from the Chinese character for "split" until the softly glowing, reddish-orange Qi element floated off the page. Though it was one of many that Clara had manifested that Wednesday morning before heading off to school, Clara looked at each one fondly as the delicate character reflected in her wondrous brown eyes.

Soon the manifested Qi element seeped into her chest, eliciting another grin. Her eyes perked up when her mother's muffled voice hollered out that breakfast was ready. She pushed herself back from her desk and plopped the ink-soaked brush into the glass of water. With care, she closed her Portal Book and slipped it into the center drawer.

With a spin on her heels, she grabbed her knapsack by its top handle, crossed the distance to the nightstand, and picked up her cell phone. She glanced at Bo Bo, her stuffed panda, on her pillow, and said, "Okay Bo Bo, you need to watch over the room now and keep the Portal Book safe. See you after school!"

Bo Bo stared back at Clara with his usual silent expression, and Clara smiled. She exited her room and bounded down the hallway. As she entered the kitchen, her father was sitting at the kitchen table, engrossed with his phone while holding a cup of coffee in his other hand. She glanced down and saw leftover scallion pancake from the previous night's dinner and her eyes lit up.

"Scallion pancake!" said Clara hungrily as she reached for one of the golden crispy triangular pieces. It was warm to the touch and her tastebuds were anticipating the crispiness of the flour pancake and the oily goodness of something fried.

"I have an early showing this morning so I didn't have time to make breakfast, so I just reheated them," said her mother. She was looking at Clara from the stove as she ladled something into a glass bowl. She smiled when she saw how happy Clara was crunching on the scallion pancake. She couldn't help but notice the pretty bamboo hair accessory that Clara used to tie her hair up into a ponytail draped over her left shoulder.

With the ladle down, she carefully touched the sides of the bowl.

Confirming it wasn't too hot, she grabbed it with both hands. She turned slowly with the glass storage bowl and placed it onto the table.

"Here's your *jook*," she said to her husband.

Clara's father looked up from his phone as his eyes gazed at the fresh rice porridge, referred to as *jook* in Cantonese. The creamy white rice glistened as slivers of meat and black chunks of preserved duck egg floated on top. Before he could thank his wife, Clara's eyes lit up as she asked, "You made *jook*?"

Her mother smiled at Clara's question as she fitted the plastic lid onto the bowl and carefully placed it into the nylon lunch bag. She then grabbed a waxed paper bag containing golden and slightly oily pieces of fried Chinese dough. She gently placed it on top of the glass Tupperware and zipped up the nylon lunch bag. As she was about to slide it along the kitchen table to her husband, she was startled when Clara eagerly grabbed it with both of her hands and pulled it towards her with a giggle, declaring, "Mine!"

"Clara!" said her mother with surprise as her father looked at Clara curiously. "That's for your father. Besides, when did you ever bring lunch to school?"

"I haven't had your *jook* in a while," said Clara playfully as she slipped on her knapsack. "Besides, you can always scoop up another bowl for *Baba*! Thanks Mom! I'm sure it will be yummy!"

As Clara turned, her father admonished her, "And don't be telling your White friends that they're one thousand-year-old eggs. It's not really a thousand years old. Or hundred years old. It's just marketing."

"They won't think that," said Clara's mother with a slight eyeroll. "Making fun of Chinese food is so old school, that doesn't happen anymore."

"Thanks, Mom," said Clara appreciatively as she looked up at her mother with a grin. "When I come home, could we practice some more Chinese?"

Her mother looked up proudly, nodded and said, "Of course."

"Great, thanks for the *jook*!" said Clara as she spun around toward the front entrance of their co-op.

"See ya later, princess," said her father as he looked back down at his phone.

Clara looked up and turned to her father, "*Baba?*"

"What's up, princess?" he asked as he looked over at her.

"Would you mind calling me 'empress' instead?"

Her father looked puzzled as he glanced up to an equally puzzled look from his wife. He looked back up and said, "Um, sure, empress."

Clara smiled as she finished slipping into her sneakers and responded enthusiastically, "Thanks, *Baba!*"

She pulled open the door and left as her two parents looked bewildered, who then burst into a shared chuckle.

TWO

The bowl of *jook* spun slowly under the glowing yellowish light of the humming microwave. Clara was salivating as the *jook* was almost ready to be devoured. Her eyes lit up as the microwave dinged, and she pressed the clunky button to pop open the door. She carefully pulled out the warm bowl and placed it onto her plastic lunch tray. She could feel the bustling of students behind her in the cafeteria as her hand closed the microwave door. With both hands on the tray, she turned around and found herself suddenly face-to-face with Clarissa, the high school bully.

In her ankle boots, blonde-haired Clarissa stood an inch or two taller than Clara. Her tight light blue sweater showed off her slender build as she stared at Clara with her arms crossed and her lunch bag dangling from her left hand. Her eyes rolled as she obnoxiously exhaled while her two cohorts stood behind her.

"Oh gross! What is that?" exclaimed Clarissa as she pointed her finger down at the bowl of warm *jook*.

Clara glanced down at the *jook* and looked up defiantly, "Something you couldn't appreciate."

Clara proceeded to sidestep her, but Clarissa, annoyed, stepped in and tried to push up the tray. But Clara anticipated the trickery and shifted away. She pulled the tray out of reach as she planted her right foot down, hooked her left foot onto Clarissa's left foot, and pulled. Clarissa clumsily fell to the floor as other students abruptly looked down at her.

Clara tried to walk away toward her friends watching her from their lunch table. A Chinese American teen boy got up, but Clara shook her head to hold him at bay when Clarissa yelled from behind, "Hey *ching chong*! Go eat your weird smelly Chinese food!"

Clara suddenly felt all eyes on her. She was never the confrontational type, always tried to ignore the countless insults from Clarissa. But that day, Clarissa, the high school bully, was talking to Empress Warrior Wu.

Clara calmly spun around and walked to within a few feet of a glaring Clarissa who had just gotten back up and she sternly said, "Hey! Chinese people never say *ching chong* because in Chinese, it means, 'I'm stupid!'"

The other students who were watching the exchange burst out in laughter as they looked at a flustered Clarissa. She beamed back at Clara and yelled out, *"Ching chong!* I'll…"

"Hey stupid!" someone blurted out toward Clarissa before she could finish her insult. Others soon chimed into a laughing chorus of, "Hey stupid!" Clarissa was speechless and suddenly turned red. She spun around, stomped away in a huff as her two friends followed.

Clara smiled as a few other students gave her approving glances. Clarissa was no *Huo Dou* Fire Demon Dog, but standing up to Clarissa felt good. Clara turned toward her friends who were all smiling at her from the lunch table. She quickened her pace because she didn't want her *jook* to get cold.

THREE

Clara fidgeted with the key in the lock, and the apartment door finally swung open. Upon entering, she slipped out of her shoes and neatly placed them in front of the shoe rack.

"I'm home," she yelled out.

"Hi Clara," her mother responded from the kitchen.

Clara bounded into the kitchen and saw that her mother had laid out materials for her Chinese lesson. She glanced up at her mother and her heart skipped a beat in happiness that she never felt before toward her Chinese lessons.

"Cool. I'm so ready for our lesson," exclaimed Clara as her mother looked up from the counter.

"I'm so happy to hear that, but give me half an hour or so, I need to finish prepping for dinner," asked her mother.

"Okay. How did the showing go?" asked Clara as she slipped off one strap of her knapsack.

"Good. I'm sure I'll get an offer soon with this crazy market," said her mother confidently.

"Great! Okay, I'll come back in a bit then," said Clara as she began to walk away and down the hall to her room.

"See you soon," said her mother as she returned to her kitchen prep work.

Clara entered her room and closed the door behind her. She glanced down at her stuffed panda and asked, "Did you keep the Portal Book safe today, Bo Bo?" said Clara teasingly as she placed her phone and house key on the nightstand. That's when she caught a faint glowing reflection in the dark plastic eyes of her stuffed panda.

Clara turned toward her desk and saw a warm glow seeping from the desk drawer. She gasped as she raced over, plopped her knapsack down, and opened the drawer. The edges of the Portal Book were indeed flashing a warm glow. She pulled it out and laid it out on her desk. She opened the Portal Book, and on the page was the Chinese character for "Return."

She grabbed her ponytail and slid her hands down its length. As she held it, she settled down into her chair and thought for a moment. It was earlier than she had anticipated. *Why was she being called back to Azen? If she were to return to Azen, would she come back in time for her Chinese lesson? But there must be a good reason*, she thought as she nodded. With a sense of urgency, she plucked out a clean brush and gently wet its bristles with black ink. She nervously turned to her door for a moment before looking back down at the Portal Book. With her left hand, she flipped to the next page and brushed out her full Chinese name.

She placed the brush back into the cup of water that held the brush from earlier that morning. She stood up, and in seconds, the fiery embers started to slither out of the black inked characters of her beautifully brushed Chinese name, *Wu Chu Hua*. Her eyes reflected the fiery glow of the book as she took a deep breath and closed her eyes just as the bright warm golden light enveloped her.

The bright light flashed in Bo Bo's dark plastic eyes, and soon it faded, leaving behind an empty chair.

FOUR

The light fully cocooned her in its bright warmth. It felt like a breeze was gently flowing over her entire body until it was no more. She could feel the tendrils of light release their hold as her feet settled firmly onto something solid. Her eyes fluttered open as she adjusted to the new scene when a familiar voice called out to her.

"Welcome back to Azen, Empress Warrior Wu," said the Guardian Panda as he stared at her with his soulful brown eyes behind the black furry patches.

Her elated expression as she ran toward the Guardian Panda was telling. He was not expecting her to bury herself in his fluffy white-and-black fur with her arms barely able to wrap around him. But despite the unexpected hug, he embraced her tenderly with his paws as a smile formed across his face.

As she pulled away from him, a panda attendant came into view on Clara's left. She bowed her snout lightly as Clara reciprocated, and that's when she noticed the shoes on top of the red pillow in the panda's arms.

"Shoes!" exclaimed Clara.

"Yes," said the Guardian Panda. "I didn't want you to go without shoes on your return to Azen. Please take them."

Clara quickly took the shoes and thanked the panda attendant.

She dropped the shoes onto the ground and slipped into them. She looked at them and remembered how she almost had to trek back to Bamboo City without shoes on her first time traveling to Azen. As she looked up, she saw the Guardian Panda looking down at her.

"Empress Warrior Wu," he began. "We have called you back here for some urgent news."

Dread sunk into Clara's chest as she asked, "Is the Warlock army already here?"

"No. Not yet," said the Guardian Panda. "But it's another matter, and we need to fly back to Bamboo Tower immediately."

Clara nodded and looked past the Guardian Panda. She could make out the outline of two cranes down the path.

"Then let's go," she said as she followed the Guardian Panda.

As they approached the cranes, the crane closest to Clara, nodded and said, "Greetings, Empress Warrior Wu. I am Shiori. I am your dedicated crane while you are here on Azen."

Clara couldn't contain her excitement at having a dedicated crane to fly. After a skip in her step, she replied, "It's very nice to meet you, Shiori."

Clara and the Guardian Panda soon mounted their cranes and harnessed themselves in. Clara couldn't miss the experience of flying atop a graceful crane and soon, the two cranes soared into the air, on their way toward Bamboo Tower for the urgent news that awaited her.

FIVE

The flight was calm, and Clara was able to let go of her teenage responsibilities back home. Knowing that time worked differently in Azen than on Earth, she didn't have to worry about her parents missing her. She trusted the Portal Book to bring her back in time for her Chinese lesson, and dinner thereafter.

She looked ahead as the warm sunbeams danced along her back as the sun started to set behind her. She took in the vast forests, green plains, and rocky formations that jutted out below. Every now and then, intriguing structures revealed themselves and she wondered what they were. *There was so much to explore*, she thought.

She felt Shiori descending and looked to her right to see her Guardian Panda atop his crane. She looked ahead and could make out the magnificence of Bamboo City.

"Hold on tight, Empress Warrior Wu," Shiori instructed.

"I will," said Clara as she gripped the harness and leaned into the crane's neck.

Clara's eyes widened and she smiled as Bamboo City started to come into view. Shiori aimed for the open hangar entrance of Bamboo Tower as she flew in behind the crane carrying the Guardian Panda. Clara felt the sudden swoosh of air as they passed through the hangar entrance and the exhilaration of the crane's wings opening wide until finally, she gracefully landed.

"We have arrived, Empress Warrior Wu," said Shiori as Clara carefully climbed off.

"Thank you!" said Clara as she walked around to the front of the crane and bowed gently. The crane looked at Clara with her beady eyes and nodded her head.

"Come now, Empress Warrior Wu," said the Guardian Panda. "The Panderess wants to welcome you back before we address the matter at hand."

Anxiety filled Clara's chest as she nodded to the Guardian Panda and followed him to the bamboo lift. He stepped into one side as she took the other. The lift rose and Clara eyed the passing scenes as each floor rushed past until they reached the floor of the Panderess. She followed the Guardian Panda while taking in the ornate décor of red columns, square-patterned bracing, and numerous illumination jades that gave the floor a bright sheen.

As they approached the center of the floor and the awaiting Panderess, Clara suddenly looked down at her jeans and light-green buttoned sweater with a t-shirt underneath and felt self-conscious.

Her hands quickly pulled her sweater taut and she wiped her palms on the back of her jeans. She straightened up her posture and made her steps more deliberate.

"Welcome back, Empress Warrior Wu," said the Panderess, whose regal aura filled the room. She was adorned in a silky buttoned red top that was stitched with intricate golden embroidery. Her hands were each tucked into the cuff of the opposite sleeve as she looked at Clara with her steady brown eyes.

"*Xie Xie*, Panderess. It is a pleasure to be back," said Clara, saying *thank you* in Mandarin while bowing to the Panderess, who did the same.

"I hope your flight here was a joyful one," said the Panderess.

"It was. Flying through the air on a crane isn't something I get to do back home," said Clara joyfully.

"I'm glad it was. I'm sure your Guardian Panda has told you that we had to request your return earlier than expected due to an urgent matter."

Clara nodded, and the Panderess continued, "Very well then. Let's go to the Jade Floor so that Empress Warrior Wu may be brought up to date."

"The Jade Floor?" asked Clara.

"Yes, it's where we manufacturer all of our jade weaponry and conduct research. We'll be meeting our top Jadeologist," said the Panderess.

"Jadeologist?" asked Clara with a baffled expression.

"I see you haven't been given the full tour of Bamboo Tower or Bamboo City," remarked the Panderess as her eyes shifted to the Guardian Panda. "Very well. Seeing that you have arrived earlier than expected, I'm sure a tour can be arranged for you. You are, of course, our Panda Empress Warrior."

Clara smiled and exclaimed, "That would be wonderful!"

"Very well, then," stated the Panderess. "Please follow me."

The Panderess quickly walked past Clara and the Guardian Panda, and she was quickly followed by two panda attendants. Clara and the Guardian Panda soon followed them and when they arrived at the descending lift, a panda attendant went in first, followed by the Panderess and the second attendant. Clara and the Guardian Panda followed and stood on the opposing side as the lift started to smoothly descend.

"Our Jadeologist is a bit eccentric, so please try to accommodate him," asked the Panderess.

"I'll try," answered Clara though she was searching through her mind for what "eccentric" meant.

The lift stopped after a few floors, and the view of the floor was basked in light green. An incessant chorus of grinding emanated from the floor as the Panderess and her attendants stepped off, followed by Clara, then the Guardian Panda.

As they walked further along the path, Clara's eyes wandered over hundreds of pandas, each adorably wearing a face mask, grinding a piece of jade with their paws against a whetstone. They were shaping jade pieces, and Clara could see that one section of pandas was grinding arrow tips, while another section was fashioning spear tips, and another was shaping them into oblong pieces.

As Clara looked over, she saw that her group had caught the attention of several pandas, who started to whisper to one another.

"Wow, they must really love seeing the Panderess," said Clara.

"On any occasion that would be true, but I think it's you they are looking at, Empress Warrior Wu," said the Guardian Panda.

Clara looked up and scanned the room as masked pandas looked up. Their paws pointed at her, and she blushed at all the attention.

"Greetings!" said a boisterous voice that was closing in, and Clara trained her eyes on a very jubilant panda waddling over to them. His white top was shedding fine green dust that must have come from the grinding of the green jade. He was wearing a mask, but it could not hide the white beard sprouting from underneath his chin. His white eyelashes bounced slightly.

"Le Le," said the Panderess as she donned a mask that was provided by one of the attendants. The other attendant provided a mask to Clara and the Guardian Panda.

"Greetings Panderess," said the Jadeologist, who then looked at Clara, "And Empress Warrior Wu, it is an honor to meet you."

"It is an honor to meet you too," said Clara as she returned his slight bow as she slipped on the mask.

"Please, follow me to the Jade Room, where we can talk about my favorite topic, jade!" said the Jadeologist excitedly.

As Clara followed the group, she observed more pandas shaping jade pieces. An overwhelming number of them were shaping the illumination jades. They approached a circular glass room as a glass door slid open. They all walked through and Clara looked in awe. She saw that along the inner perimeter of the glass room were a number of pandas working with different shapes of jade. In the middle was a large bamboo table with a host of jade pieces, some still its raw form, some half shaped, others cracked open. Her eyes smiled as they spied the Bow of Destiny resting on a bamboo stand.

The Jadeologist removed his mask along with everyone else as an attendant collected them.

"Welcome to the glorious Jade Room, Empress Warrior Wu. This is where I spend most of my time," exclaimed the Jadeologist. "Please, this way."

"He's quite happy," Clara whispered to the Guardian Panda, who responded, "We think it's the jade dust."

Clara giggled as they made their way to the Bow of Destiny.

As the group approached, the attendants fell away from the Panderess, who walked a few steps behind the Jadeologist. Le Le gestured for Clara to step forward. Clara nodded and stepped up to the circular table. He settled his big furry feet, looked down at her, and smiled.

"Oh, this is so exciting! To be talking to you, Empress Warrior Wu!" he said as Clara smiled. "Well, let me tell you everything. When I heard the news that the Bamboo Jade shattered, from the bite of a *Huo Dou* Fire Demon Dog, I was in utter disbelief. Disbelief. I tell you! How could the Bamboo Jade, that has been in the possession of the Panda Kingdom since its acquisition, be destroyed? But then I saw the jade shards and examined each piece myself. No one knows the Bamboo Jade better than me. I along with many jadelogists before me have examined the Bamboo Jade for centuries trying to understand how it derives its power. But to no avail. So, when I put it back together, I could see that it was futile. It no longer had its exquisite power. And my heart was shattered too. But then I was told that your jade bracelet came to life and powered up all the green jades in its proximity! 'Impossible!' I thought! I could not believe it, but then I looked at all of our green jade, they were all glowing mysteriously. There is no other explanation!"

The Jadeologist picked up a whole raw jade nearby and held it out in front of Clara, who could see that it was slightly glowing. He placed it back down and continued.

"So, I immediately studied your jade bracelet and was amazed that it was indeed, imbued with the powerful force that powers all our green jade. How exciting! But exciting as it may be, it should not be. No earthen jade should be able to power the jade here on Azen."

Clara raised her hand, and the Jadeologist stopped. He looked down at her and blinked, "Yes?"

"Has it ever been tried?" asked Clara.

The Jadeologist looked stupefied. He looked up at the rest of the pandas who also had a blank stare.

"You're right! There has never been an opportunity for us to use an earthen jade to power up our Azen green jade. We never needed to," remarked the Jadeologist.

"But upon further inspection," continued the Jadelogist as he gripped the bow and laid it flat on the edge of the table as he maneuvered a large glass lens over it. "If you look through this magnifying lens, you'll see that there are microfractures in your jade bracelet."

Clara looked through the lens that magnified the jade bracelet greatly and for the first time, she could see the intricate shades of green that coalesced in her beautiful jade bracelet. Every now and then, she could see shimmers of white light racing within the jade itself, but to her dismay, she did see the small cracks in the jade. She pulled away and looked back at the Jadeologist.

"I have examined the Bamboo Jade myself countless times, and it never exhibited these types of microfractures. As amazing that your earthen jade has the Azen power, I'm afraid it's temporary. It is my belief that in another battle, where so much pressure would be put onto this earthen jade, that it would shatter and leave our panda soldiers defenseless."

Clara nodded glumly, and the Jadeologist asked, "If you don't mind me asking Empress Warrior Wu, where did you get your jade bracelet?"

"My mother. She gave it to me when I was ten years old. She has one too and told me that her mother had given her one. And should I be so lucky to have a daughter one day, I can carry on with the tradition and give her one as well."

"I see. And where did your mother get the one that she gave to you?"

"Oh, from Hong Kong. I'm pretty sure it was made in China, though," said Clara.

"I see. So, it is Chinese jade," said the Jadeologist ponderingly. "Though this is the first time I have ever had the opportunity to examine earthen jade, and as amazing as it is that your jade bracelet has its power, I'm afraid it will not survive the next battle."

Clara grimly looked up and asked, "What can we do?"

"We must find a new Bamboo Jade," said the Jadeologist.

There was a moment of silence and Clara asked, "And where do we find that?"

The Jadelogist paused, looked at the Panderess and the Guardian Panda, who were silent. He turned to Clara and said ominously, "The Jade Labyrinth."

SIX

"Over a millennium ago," the Panderess started, "We didn't always have the power of the Bamboo Jade to aid us on our battles with the Warlock and his hordes of demon creatures. Nor did the other kingdoms. But we had the power of the Qi element invoked by our Panda Warriors, who were summoned by the Portal Books."

"With the warriors leading us into battle with hundreds of determined battle pandas, we fought relentlessly along with the fellow kingdoms. And though we were victorious each time, we incurred staggering losses. Each loss decimated our panda ranks, and it took a toll on the panda population.

It came to a point in the battles that our panda population fell dangerously low, as we don't reproduce as quickly as other kingdoms. We were on the verge of extinction if we didn't remove ourselves from battle. But doing so would have left the other kingdoms to bear the onslaught of the Warlock armies. And if their numbers became decimated by the evil Warlock creatures, their populations would suffer the same fate and leave the Portal Books to possibly fall into the Warlock's hands. That we could not allow.

Emperor Warrior Hong, our summoned Panda Emperor Warrior at that time, was a loyal and devoted emperor warrior, and he saw the hopelessness of our declining panda population. He knew that there were mystical forces at work on Azen as the Portal Books possessed the power that allowed him to manifest and invoke the Qi element of the earth Wu. He was determined to find a way to protect us all.

He went directly to the Portal Books and brushed frantically into the books for help, but there was no response. He resorted to yelling in vain at the books, pleading for help. Again, no response. But he never gave up. And one late evening, exhausted by his exhortations, he fell asleep at the base of the column of his Portal Book. He awoke to the flipping pages of the Portal Book, and when he stood up, the pages were aglow, and he saw it was open to a blank page.

As he stared at the blank page, a fiery image of a mountain glowed. He continued to stare when an oblong object floated off the page, and he realized it was a piece of jade. He also recognized the mountain. It was Jade Mountain, which we had always mined for illumination jades. You must understand, prior to the discovery of green, blue, red, white, and silver jade, we had only the clear jade that provided us with light. That was plentiful.

The emperor warrior went directly to his Guardian Panda at that time, and they both went to the Panderor, who reigned over our kingdom. The Emperor Warrior Hong told the Panderor what the Portal Book had shown him. They had nothing to lose, so he, the Guardian Panda, and two of the best battle pandas traveled to Jade Mountain. There wasn't anything unusual about this as all the kingdom animals mined the mountain for illumination jades. Except for one oddity.

A long time before then, a cave entrance had been discovered in the course of mining. A number of kingdom animals went in to explore it, but none ever returned. But something odd happened one day. A reclusive order of the Azen monks, consisting of members of all the kingdoms, suddenly appeared one day, paying silent homage to the mysterious cave entrance. They stayed there for days. At the same time, because of the number of miners who went in to investigate and never returned, the Kingdom Council feared that the monks would enter the mysterious cave entrance. So they then ordered by Azen decree that no one shall ever enter that cave ever again. But when miners went back to seal the cave, all the monks had disappeared. It was only logical that they had done what the Kingdom Council had feared. They all had gone into the cave and suffered the same fate. Therefore, it was sealed off. Inscriptions were carved into the stone face itself to warn all would-be explorers that no one was to ever enter the cave entrance ever again.

But the Emperor Warrior Hong felt strongly that the cave entrance was where he was to go in search of some unknown jade stone. When they arrived at the sealed-off cave, the Guardian Panda ordered the seal to be broken. Once it was broken, a cold, stale wind emanated from the cave that pierced even our thick fur. The battle pandas at that time said it was like a spirit had flown right through them.

The Guardian Panda implored the emperor warrior to let him go with him, but he rejected his plea. Emperor Warrior Hong said he must go alone. Armed only with a regular bow, as the Bow of Destiny did not yet exist; his quiver, and an illumination jade torch, he bravely disappeared into the dark void. According to the pandas, it was almost as if the mist within the cave swallowed him up.

The Guardian Panda and the two battle pandas waited hours, then a day, and finally, at the end of the second day, just as the worried Guardian Panda was about to enter the cave himself to search for Emperor Warrior Hong, he appeared out of nowhere. When he stepped over the cave threshold, he looked haggard, but there was a smile on his face as he looked up at the Guardian Panda.

Before the Guardian Panda could ask what had happened, the emperor warrior held out a large green jade. It was the first time that any panda had laid eyes on a green jade, though Emperor Warrior Hong had told us they were plentiful in your world, in China. A pure white light suddenly spiraled out and flashed in front of everyone. To everyone's amazement, the emperor warrior smiled and boldly walked to where all the mine tunnels were. He approached each tunnel entrance with the green jade stretched out in front of him. After passing a few tunnel entrances, the green jade flashed gently, and he entered that tunnel. The Guardian Panda and the two battle pandas followed.

The other panda miners followed him until he stopped. He looked all around, and the tunnel walls were filled with clear illumination jades. He waved the green jade around until its glow pointed straight down. He smiled and asked the miners to dig downward. The panda miners were confused, but the Guardian Panda insisted, and the panda miners did as they were told. The emperor warrior then said he needed to be taken to the Bamboo of Eternity.

The Bamboo of Eternity is the name of the one bamboo stalk that we believe to be the original bamboo that gave rise to all Azen bamboo. We knew that there was something special about this one bamboo stalk because it was so large. It also had one distinct difference: It was not green, but had a golden yellowish hue.

We considered this bamboo to be sacred and we honor it to this day. Before it was honored and deemed sacred, we took from this one bamboo to spin bamboo thread from it. Some of the finest clothing for honored ceremonies was woven from it. We created some intricate artwork from it as well. But as it was the only one, we limited harvesting from its beautiful stalk, which magically regrew.

That day though, the emperor warrior arrived at the Bamboo of Eternity. He went alone to stand in front of it as the Guardian Panda and the battle pandas watched. The emperor warrior didn't say much as he walked along the perimeter of the bamboo stalk until he found a spot. He pressed his hand against it, and something made him nod. He placed the green jade against it, and a momentous flash of light appeared. A light that the pandas had never seen before from the Bamboo of Eternity.

When the light vanished, he waved the pandas over. You can imagine how nervous the pandas were. The emperor warrior calmed them, and he asked that a section of bamboo be harvested. The Guardian Panda did so without question and asked a couple of pandas to harvest a piece of bamboo. Once they removed the piece of bamboo, the emperor warrior asked to be taken back to Bamboo Tower.

Once there, he asked for Bamboo City's finest bamboo artisan, whom the Panderor summoned. The emperor warrior explained to the artisan what he needed, and the artisan said he'd work through the night if he had to. And he indeed worked through the night. The next morning, he presented to the emperor warrior a beautiful bamboo bow, hewn from the Bamboo of Eternity.

When the emperor warrior admired it, the Guardian Panda asked about the hollow above the grip. The emperor warrior smiled and asked to be taken to their top jadesmith. We didn't have a Jadeologist at the time.

As the Guardian Panda introduced the emperor warrior to their most talented jadesmith, they talked extensively. Emperor Warrior Hong showed her the hollow of the bow and the green jade, which she looked at in awe. Once the jadesmith understood what was being asked of her, the emperor warrior handed the jadesmith both the bow and the green jade. She looked them both over, nodded and took them back to her place of work. She said she needed at least the day and expected to return by evening.

Later that evening, the emperor warrior and the Guardian Panda returned, and the jadesmith was jovial. She said the shaping and polishing of the jade went according to expectations. She handed both the bow and the newly shaped and polished green jade back to the emperor warrior. He smiled upon seeing the gleaming green jade. As the jadesmith and Guardian Panda watched, the emperor warrior gently inserted the green jade into the hollow of the hewn bamboo bow. It snapped in as if they were meant to be joined, and another brilliant flash of light radiated out. At that moment, the Bow of Destiny was brought to life.

Emperor Warrior Hong spoke to the jadesmith once more and told the Guardian Panda that they needed to return to Jade Mountain. Upon their return, they were greeted with excitement. A panda miner led both the emperor warrior and the Guardian Panda to the mine tunnel, where they were greeted by a wagon partially full of green jade. The miners explained that as soon as they had begun digging in the spot where the emperor warrior had indicated, they started finding green jade. Though they had only dug down about ten feet, the green jade seemed plentiful. Emperor Warrior Hong picked up a few thick pieces, which all glowed slightly. He smiled and said they needed to return to the jadesmith with a few pieces of green jade.

Once they returned to the jadesmith, she was eager to take the green jade and told them to return in a few hours. Upon their return, she handed to the emperor warrior ten pieces of green jade shaped into arrow heads and five small oblong pieces. He smiled and thanked her. He asked the Guardian Panda to take him to the battle training area in Bamboo City.

The emperor warrior and the Guardian Panda rushed to the training area. Excitedly, the emperor warrior picked up a quiver of bows. He replaced ten metal arrowheads with the ten jade arrowheads. With the Guardian Panda and many panda archers watching, he walked not fifty feet from the target but one hundred feet. He took out one of the glowing jade-tipped arrows, aimed, and released it at the target. To everyone's awe, it hit the target on center. Though impressive to hit a bull's eye at one hundred feet, he was the Panda Warrior, so the battle archers were not entirely surprised. The emperor warrior took out another jade-tipped arrow, aimed it, and released it. It split the shaft of the first embedded arrow. Such a feat was almost impossible, and this time his marksmanship surprised everyone.

He asked for the best panda archer to step forward and asked him to try to split his arrow. The panda archer looked uncertain, but he did as he was asked. After three attempts using arrows from his quiver, he hit the target but did not split or hit Emperor Warrior Hong's arrow. The Emperor Warrior then gave him a jade-tipped arrow, which the panda archer marveled at. He aimed, released it, and the jade-tipped arrow split the shaft of the emperor warrior's arrow. The panda archer was in awe, and when he was asked to do it again, he did so effortlessly.

The emperor warrior explained that the one Bamboo Jade was the all-powerful jade that gave accuracy to any green jade-tipped arrow. He also explained that when a jade is joined with battle armor crafted from the Bamboo of Eternity, it would become impervious to attacks. The Guardian Panda asked how the emperor warrior knew this. The emperor warrior said that he was shown this while he was in the cave.

The Guardian Panda sent for the Panderor, who listened to the emperor warrior describing the newfound powers of the green jade. He watched the demonstration of the jade arrow's accuracy. They took one of the oblong jade pieces and embedded it into the royal armor that had been hewn from the Bamboo of Eternity. The battle armor was then placed on a battle panda, who to his utter surprise was then able to absorb a blow from the Guardian Panda's staff. After a few more directed blows, the Panderor saw the immediate benefits and by decree, ordered the mining of the green jade and the mass production of the bamboo battle armor to be made from the Bamboo of Eternity.

Emperor Warrior Hong rejoined his fellow emperor and empress warriors. At that time, it was during a five lunar moon cycle. After he told them of his journey, he told them that there was a jade waiting for each of them to discover to aid their own kingdom. They all rushed back to Jade Mountain.

Each warrior went in separately, and though it only felt like a few hours for some of them, it was anywhere from one to two days before they all returned. The water Wu Warrior went in second and came back with a blue jade, which is now the Claw Jade. The air Wu Warrior came back with a white jade, which is now the Moon Jade. The fire Wu Warrior came back with a red jade, which is now the Horn Jade. And lastly, the metal Wu Warrior came back with a silver jade, which is now the Kinetic Jade.

They each knew exactly what they needed to do once they emerged from the cave. That was how the Claw Staff, the Club Horn of *Kting Voar*, the Moon Star *Shuriken*, and the Kinetic Sword all came about.

Each weapon gave to its warrior reliable new protection, but the jade's most important gift was the extra layer of impregnability for our armor. Over time, the silken bamboo mesh armor was interwoven with Clawdium fibers, which made it even stronger. With successive battles, more jade was mined and embedded into more armor. Once the armor was protected, it lasted for generations. Our warriors usually wear battle armor that has been in their families for generations," said the Panderess as she finished her oratory.

"That is amazing," said a stupefied Clara, spellbound by the Panderess' story.

"That was how the tide of impending destruction of the kingdoms was turned by the discovery of the power of the jade. But now, after centuries, we may be the first kingdom to be potentially defenseless against the Warlock's creatures. Perhaps the first green jade had reached its time, as it is very old," lamented the Panderess.

Clara looked at the Bow of Destiny and the jade bracelet that her mother had given her, which was fitted snugly above the bow's grip. She looked up at the Panderess, then her Guardian Panda and asked, "What do you need me to do?"

The Guardian Panda looked at her starkly, "You'll need to venture into the Forbidden Cave of Jade Mountain."

SEVEN

After changing into her training attire, Clara wrapped her arms around her drawn-up knees and tucked her chin into them as she felt the void in her stomach gradually expand. Her eyes were drawn toward the edge of her bed as she braced herself against the pillow propped against the bamboo headboard.

A flutter of the wind drew her eyes upwards toward the open bamboo shutters as a crane with a panda passed by. She rocked a bit in place, waiting for her dinner as she looked down at the Bow of Destiny and its quiver full of jade-tipped arrows.

She let out a deep breath and reached out for the bow, resting the grip with her jade bracelet across her knees. She stared at its deep green color and wondered how her jade bracelet possessed the power to command all the green jade within the panda army. But she struggled as uncertain thoughts swirled through her mind about its mysterious power, why it was temporary, and how it could fail the Panda Kingdom.

"What makes you so special?" Clara muttered. A knock at the door made her look up.

"Empress Warrior Wu," said the Guardian Panda as he came in followed by another panda attendant, who bowed slightly and placed a tray onto the table.

"Hi, Guardian Panda," said Clara as she put the bow down and turned her head toward the other panda. She watched the panda attendant set down the tray with what looked like bamboo noodles, topped with vegetables, along with an egg and a cup of tea. The panda attendant bowed slightly and retreated.

"How are you, Empress Warrior Wu?" asked the Guardian Panda.

"I'm okay, I guess," said Clara as her voice trailed off.

The Guardian Panda came closer as his thick white-and-black fur bounced. With his brown eyes, he beamed down at her and asked, "Is something wrong, Empress Warrior Wu?"

With her head turned upward she asked, "What happens if I can't find the green jade?"

The Guardian Panda blinked and soon settled down onto the floor. Even seated, he was so large he was at eye level with Clara. "You will, Empress Warrior Wu, for you are the Panda Warrior."

"But what's inside the cave that prevented the other pandas from returning? Did Emperor Warrior Hong say anything about what I am supposed to do?" asked Clara anxiously.

His blank stare told all: He did not know. "I can only tell you that he said, 'Remain true.'"

"What is that supposed to mean?"

He blinked and simply said, "I don't know. But seeing that all the warriors of that time all came back with a jade in hand, it has to be something that only an empress or emperor warrior can achieve."

"I see," said Clara before she asked. "But what happens if there is only one jade that controls them all and no more?"

"If there is only one," said the Guardian Panda before he looked down momentarily. "Then we will deal with our fate."

Clara nodded pensively as she rested her chin on her knees and stared off.

"Are you not hungry?" asked the Guardian Panda.

Clara turned her head and could smell the aroma of the delicate broth and returned her head back onto her knees. "Maybe later," Clara responded as she suddenly felt bloated, suppressing any hunger she may have had.

The Guardian Panda stared at his empress warrior and saw the uncertainty in her eyes. Past warriors did not divulge much of their experience in the Forbidden Cave of Jade Mountain, and the kingdoms were forced to have faith that whatever lay in the cave was for the empress and emperor warriors only.

"How would you like to take a short tour around Bamboo City?" asked the Guardian Panda.

Clara's eyes lit up as she turned toward the Guardian Panda, "Really?"

"Yes," he said, realizing that Clara needed a distraction. "Take the Bow of Destiny with you and let me show you our great city."

Once the lift landed on the ground floor, Clara smiled as she stepped off with the Guardian Panda. She looked at the large bamboo stalks reaching into the dark navy sky as illumination jades let off a soft light upon each section of the bamboo stalks.

"Let me tell you how we identify each of the bamboo stalks in Bamboo City. Bamboo Tower is the beginning, and it is only designated by one number, the floor," explained the Guardian Panda. "So, if you are ever given an address with one number, it's always the floor of Bamboo Tower."

"How many floors are there?" asked Clara.

The Guardian Panda twisted around and upward and pointed, "Sixty-eight."

Looking up with her head tilted as far back as it could go, Clara could only say, "Wow."

The Guardian Panda continued, "See this wide stone path that we are on? This is The Meridian, and each ringed path that flows out and around Bamboo Tower increments by one. The closest ring is simply one and going clockwise, the first bamboo stalk is one and so on. The last number is the floor of that bamboo stalk. So, Empress Warrior Wu, if I needed you to go to three-four-five, how would you find it?"

Clara smiled and looked back at the imposing Bamboo Tower before she returned her gaze down The Meridian, which led all the way down to the perimeter of The Ring, the remnant of an outer wall of a once-massive bamboo that now guarded Bamboo City. She looked right at the third ringed path and counted the four bamboo stalks to the right. Looking up, she counted five floors up and pointed.

"Third ring, four bamboo stalks over, and the fifth floor?" she asked cautiously.

"You are correct," said the Guardian Panda. "Pretty easy if I may say so myself."

"That is easy," said Clara who looked to the left and asked, "But if the numbers go clockwise and around all of Bamboo Tower, then the numbers on the left can get pretty high?"

"That's true," responded the Guardian Panda, who started to walk ahead as Clara followed. "The outer rings, because they are so much larger, have bamboo stalks that number well into the hundreds."

"Wow, that's a lot of bamboo," Clara said. She noticed that each area framed by four bamboo stalks revealed a different part of panda city life. The first area on the right was a park where panda families were playing. She noticed that as she caught the attention of the pandas, many would look up and discreetly point at her. If they made eye contact with her, they would all bow slightly, and she did the same in return.

"Why is everyone bowing to me?" asked Clara.

The Guardian Panda looked down with a smile and simply said, "Because you are our Panda Empress Warrior."

Clara suddenly blushed. She'd never attracted so much attention in her life, let alone from adorable pandas. But as they started to walk down The Meridian, she heard a rush of padded feet behind her and was met by an adorable toddler panda. Clara's mouth fell open, and she bent down with her hands atop her knees.

The little panda, who was about the size of a small child, held a slim bamboo stalk in its mouth. It stopped about a foot away, stood up on its haunches and removed the slim bamboo stalk, which had a small leaf at the end. "Empress Warrior Wu, this is for you!" the little panda said.

Clara's heart melted as she smiled back at the adorable panda. She took the dainty bamboo stalk as the panda's parents waddled up from behind.

"Our apologies, Empress Warrior Wu and Guardian Panda. Our daughter just wanted to meet the empress warrior," said the father. The mother gently placed her paws on her daughter's shoulders.

"Oh, it's no trouble at all, I'm grateful," said Clara. "Is this for me?"

The toddler panda nodded her head, "It's for long life, that's what my parents tell me."

Clara smiled, "Well, thank you. What is your name?"

The panda looked up and gleefully said, "Ping Ping!"

"Well Ping Ping, I will make sure I will water it each day so it'll grow each day," Clara said with a smile.

"Okay," said Ping Ping bashfully as her mother padded her shoulders gently. She then said, "Thank you for accepting this gift, we'll let you get going now. Please have a good night."

Clara put her palm outward and Ping Ping looked at it awkwardly until Clara motioned it in an arc-like fashion. Ping Ping smiled and high-fived Clara with her paw and let out a snorty giggle.

Clara straightened up and bowed to Ping Ping's parents, who turned around and walked away. Ping Ping gave Clara one more glance before turning away.

"That was so cute!" said Clara as she continued the walk with the Guardian Panda.

"Let's go to two-three-one," said the Guardian Panda.

Clara followed as they entered the ground floor of the third bamboo stalk. She noticed that each bamboo stalk's ground level sat atop the intersection of each ring and radial, creating four entrances. She looked around and realized they were in a gift shop of sorts. Several pandas looked up surprised at the sight of the Panda Empress Warrior and offered a bow, which Clara returned.

"This is a crafts shop. We have some gifted artisans here. Why don't you see if there is anything that you may like?"

"Oh cool!" said Clara excitedly as she perused the bins of trinkets. There were small illumination jades in all shapes and sizes. Some were encased in a bamboo sheath while others twisted open. She came across several planted bamboo stems and she was tickled at how some resembled the ones in her own New York City Chinatown. Then she came across several bamboo medallions. They were etched with a name on one side and on the other, a carved image of a Chinese person. One bamboo medallion bore the name Hong. She then realized the medallions were the names of the Chinese Panda Emperor and Empress Warriors that came before her, and she was suddenly excited. She dug through them and saw faces of many young handsome Chinese teenaged boys and several pretty Chinese teenaged girls as well. But her eyes lit up when she came across the one she wanted to find: Hua Mulan. She picked it up and admired her young face and thought about her courage.

"Hua Mulan," said the Guardian Panda. "One of the greatest empress warriors to have fought with us."

"Totally," Clara said admiringly. "How much?"

The Guardian Panda gave a quizzical expression and said, "What do you mean?"

"How much is this?" asked Clara.

"There is no cost here, Empress Warrior Wu," said the Guardian Panda. "Besides, what would you pay with?"

"ApplePay… oh wait," said Clara as she giggled in embarrassment. For a moment, she'd forgotten where she was.

"What is this apple pay?" asked the Guardian Panda.

"Never mind," said Clara playfully. "It's how we pay for things at home."

"I see," said the Guardian Panda. "Apples must be valuable on your world."

Clara laughed as her eyes smiled humorously and said, "No no, it's not like that."

"I see. Here in Bamboo City, everyone has a role and contributes to our society. We take only what we need. Some pandas are farmers, some are battle pandas, others are artisans, scholars, and cooks."

"Wow, that is so, peaceful," said Clara. "But still, may I thank the owner if I want to take these and the small illumination jade?"

Clara's head suddenly turned to a boisterous voice from behind from a jolly panda. He exclaimed after a quick nod, "There is no need to thank me! Whatever the Panda Empress Warrior wants, you may have."

Clara assumed he was the owner and nodded and said *thank you* in

Cantonese, "*Dò Jeh.* You are very kind."

"Soon, we'll have ones made of you!" said the store owner.

Clara's stomach suddenly tightened and let out an embarrassing growl. Her hands instinctively covered her stomach as she looked up at the Guardian Panda.

The Guardian Panda nodded at the store owner and said, "I know a great place for dumplings—Divine Dumplings at three-five-one."

Clara quickly nodded to the store owner and followed the Guardian Panda out, crossed over to the third ring, and entered the fifth bamboo stalk. As she entered the eatery, all the pandas indulging in their delectable meals suddenly looked at her. They all nodded, and Clara did the same. She promptly followed the Guardian Panda to an open table and sat down. The Guardian Panda's eyebrow crooked upward as he looked at Clara, who looked awkwardly up at him. Her head barely reached over the table. He chuckled and realized that she was sitting in a chair made for pandas, and with their shorter legs, the seats of their chairs were lower to the ground.

"Empress Warrior Wu," he asked. "Please stand while we make this right for you."

As Clara rose from the low chair, a panda waiter came over and placed a bamboo block over her chair. Clara looked down at it with amusement and asked, "Is this a booster seat?"

The Guardian Panda looked confused as he replied, "It's for panda toddlers so that they may reach the table."

Clara laughed as she said to herself, "I'm sitting in a booster seat!"

After she sat down in the boosted chair, she set her trinkets down. The delicious smells of the eatery entered her nostrils and suddenly, her appetite was awakened.

"What would you like?" asked the Guardian Panda.

"Anything is fine. I trust you to order," Clara replied.

"Very well," said the Guardian Panda as he waved down a waitress, who looked over at them with her lit eyes.

The panda waitress strode over and bowed, "Guardian Panda and Empress Warrior Wu, it is my pleasure to serve you today."

Clara looked up appreciatively and responded, "*Xie Xie!* I'm looking forward to trying your dumplings!"

The Guardian Panda looked at the panda waitress and proceeded to order in Mandarin, *one leek and bamboo dumpling – "yi ge jiu cai san xian jiao zi," one cabbage and bamboo dumpling – "yi ge bai cai san xian jiao zi," and one pea, carrot, and bamboo dumpling, "yi ge san xian jiao zi."*

"Whoa! Your Mandarin is awesome!" said Clara in awe.

The Guardian Panda smiled, "Of course. I am a Chinese panda. We all speak our respective languages. The Guardian Tiger's Korean is very eloquent."

"So cool! I just never expected a panda to speak Mandarin," said Clara.

"Or speak at all from the first time we met," said the Guardian Panda playfully as Clara laughed with him.

"I get to practice my Mandarin then," said Clara with a grin.

"I noticed you also speak Cantonese," said the Guardian Panda.

"Yah, I just switch it up every now and then," said Clara playfully. "Cantonese is my first Chinese language, but I'm trying to be fluent in Mandarin too."

"I see," said the Guardian Panda. "Then I will switch it up with you to help you practice."

Clara let out a giggle and smiled at her Guardian Panda.

Her eyes wandered about the eatery as she observed the various pandas just going about their night. There were single pandas plopping dumplings into their mouths, panda couples, and panda parents trying to get their wayward panda cubs to eat a dumpling. It was simply a restaurant full of pandas eating dumplings with chopsticks.

Not a few minutes had passed when the panda waitress came back with a tray with three bamboo steamer baskets and two cups of tea. She quickly placed the stack on the table, effortlessly lifted off the lid and split the bamboo steamer baskets to reveal three types of dumplings. She put down the bamboo cups of tea and pointed to the chopsticks and napkins on the table. "Please enjoy, and it was a pleasure serving you, Empress Warrior Wu!" said the waitress.

Clara smiled back and said, "*Xie Xie*," and the waitress smiled and waddled happily away.

"Please Empress Warrior Wu, enjoy," said the Guardian Panda invitingly.

Clara smiled, grabbed a pair of chopsticks, and delicately picked up a dumpling. With one bite, her eyes lit up as she tasted the freshness of the leek and bamboo filling. The dumpling dough was just the right thickness, and it was not too hot nor too cold. Her happiness was obvious, and the Guardian Panda plucked a pair of chopsticks to enjoy the dumplings as well.

They ate in silence aside from it being punctuated by sounds of delight from Clara as she tried the other two dumplings. When she took a sip of the tea, she noticed the different but subtle flavor of bamboo. She pointed to the cup as she looked up at the Guardian Panda, "Bamboo tea leaves?"

The Guardian Panda smiled back and said, "Bamboo is life."

Clara giggled and continued to gorge on the dumplings in front of her.

As they neared the end of their dumpling feast, she rubbed her stomach in satisfaction as the Guardian Panda asked, "Do you have any more questions about tomorrow, Empress Warrior Wu?"

Clara swallowed her last bite and gently wiped her mouth as she looked up. "So, I should just trust myself."

"Yes."

"And 'remain true' is all Emperor Warrior Hong said?" asked Clara.

"Yes," said the Guardian Panda plainly.

Clara nodded her head, looked down before looking back at the Guardian Panda. "Can the other warriors go with me?"

The Guardian Panda eyes blinked momentarily. "They each have their jades already, and my assumption is that they will be okay. But the warrior in me tells me that we should limit the risk. Empress Warrior Satoh is the only warrior that commands the winged element of our combined air forces, so she cannot go. I would choose between Emperor Warrior Kim or Nguyen."

"I see," said Clara. "Okay, let me think about who I want to go with me."

"Does that mean that you're ready to go into the Forbidden Cave?"

Clara looked about her again and saw all the pandas around her. They would be counting on her. Then her heart melted once more at the panda cubs. She looked at the Guardian Panda, "Yes. I'm ready to enter the Forbidden Cave of Jade Mountain."

EIGHT

It was sunny the next day, and the Portal Circle was quiet. Clara, in her training attire, waited by her glowing Portal Book along with the Guardian Panda. By the other Portal Books, the agile white tiger, the swift-red-crowned crane, and the mighty water buffalo all stood by them. A couple of attendants from their kingdoms stood behind each of them.

The Guardian Panda looked up at the sky momentarily and with his head level once more, he simply said, "Fellow guardians, let's summon your Azen warriors."

The Guardian Tiger nodded and straightened up over the water Wu Portal Book. He picked up the Clawdium brush in his paw and wrote in Korean, "*return*." Fiery embers swirled within the black Korean word until it glowed steadily. As the glow reflected in his eyes, he settled back onto all four paws and circled off to the side of the Portal Book.

With the Horn Brush held with his cloven hoof, the mighty Guardian Buffalo hunched over the fire Wu Portal Book and wrote in Vietnamese, "*return*." He placed the brush back onto the stone tablet and watched as the fiery embers began to glow. He pushed back from the tablet as his two front hooves clattered lightly on the stone Portal Circle and he too, walked off to the side.

Finally, the Guardian Crane gently snapped up the red feathered brush in her beak and swiftly brushed out the Japanese characters for "*return*." The black characters were soon aglow as well, and the crane put the red feathered brush back. She then walked off to the side.

"Now we wait," said the Guardian Panda.

"I always tire of this part," said the Guardian Tiger as he lowered his white-and-black striped body onto the Portal Circle stone as his tailed flapped from side-to-side.

"Did you have to wait long for me?" asked Clara as she looked up at the Guardian Panda.

"Not too long, Empress Warrior Wu," he said. "About an hour. It all depends on if you are near the Portal Book in your world."

"I see. Can I look at the other Portal Books?"

"Certainly, but stand away from the front as that is where your fellow warrior would appear," admonished the Guardian Panda.

"Gotcha," said Clara as she carefully approached Sung's Portal Book. Though she had seen her share of black-inked Asian languages aglow in fiery embers, this was the first time she had seen ones brushed by the Guardians of Azen.

"My *Hangul* is pretty good, Empress Warrior Wu," said the Guardian Tiger assuredly.

Clara chuckled and nodded. "Yes, it looks perfect, Guardian Tiger," said Clara as she walked over to Yuka's Portal Book.

The Guardian Crane was hard to miss as she towered over her, but Clara smiled and addressed her, "Hello, Guardian Crane."

"Hello, Empress Warrior Wu. I am happy to see you again," she said.

"Me too," replied Clara. But before she could leave, the fiery embers glowed brighter, and the Guardian Crane requested Clara to step back.

Clara took a few steps back and watched as the Japanese characters glowed wondrously until a bright golden light engulfed the Portal Book. Clara turned her head momentarily and as the warm light faded away, Yuka's back came into full view. She was wearing a white blouse, tucked into a navy skirt with knee-high socks. Her hands found the edge of the stone tablet as she blinked a few times and perked up when she heard, "Yuka!"

She turned and saw Clara smiling and enthusiastically coming toward her. "Clara!" Yuka exclaimed with a smile and a slight bow. Clara ignored this, instead embracing the unsuspecting Yuka, who welcomed the embrace with giddiness. As they pulled back from each other, they each held each other's hands slightly.

Yuka then noticed the Guardian Crane's shadow, turned upward and with reverence, she uttered, "*Ohayo gozaimasu*, Guardian Crane!"

But she quickly looked at Clara and asked, "It's morning, right?"

Clara giggled and nodded excitedly. Yuka smiled as the Guardian Crane, responded back, "*Ohayo gozaimasu*. It is good to see you once again, Empress Warrior Satoh."

As Yuka straightened herself up, she turned around and respectfully bowed to each of the other guardians.

"Empress Warrior Satoh," said the Guardian Crane to catch Yuka's attention as she turned to her. She was greeted by a crane attendant holding a pillow, held up at its corners with braided cords, in its beak.

"Shoes!" said Yuka as she gently removed them from the pillow and the crane attendant scurried out of the way.

"They remembered this time," said Clara with a smile.

"Did you know that we were gone for only thirty minutes when we were here on Azen?" asked Yuka as she finished slipping into the second shoe.

"Yes! It was so weird to be back to almost the same time when we first vanished from our homes," said Clara. "But so cool!"

"Yes… cool!" said Yuka. "But why are we back so soon?"

"All will be explained once the other warriors have materialized from the Portal Books," said the Guardian Panda from behind as Yuka nodded.

"Are you hungry, Empress Warrior Satoh?" asked the Guardian Crane.

Yuka nodded and turned back to Clara.

"We can go back to the meal table for an early lunch while…" said the Guardian Crane before Clara raised her hand and caused her to pause.

"Guardian Crane, would it be all right if Yuka and I eat here while we wait for the boys? I'd like to be here when they appear," asked Clara.

The Guardian Crane's beady eyes blinked and looked over at the Guardian Panda, who nodded. "Certainly, that would be no trouble at all."

"*Domo arigato*," said Yuka as Clara responded with, "*Xie Xie*."

Clara and Yuka sat crossed legged from each other as they ate and talked over their snack. They traded and tasted each other's food while the guardians also ate their own. As they were finishing up, the fire Wu Portal Book became ablaze in a warm bright light and once it faded, Daniel's slender frame appeared in its place. His hair was damp and he wore a white t-shirt and a pair of red shorts with white double stripes down the sides.

He was momentarily disoriented, but his ears perked up upon hearing his name. He turned and saw Clara and Yuka waving to him. He waved back, but turned toward the Guardian Buffalo, whose massive size caught his attention out of the corner of his eye.

"Guardian Buffalo," Daniel said as the Guardian Buffalo responded, "Emperor Warrior Nguyen. It is good to see you again."

"What a trip," said Daniel as a buffalo attendant approached him with a pair of shoes on a pillow. "Oh, shoes!"

Yuka whispered to Clara and gestured subtly to the back of Daniel's toned calves and said, "Hairy."

Clara giggled and said, "Must be his other half."

"Must be," said Yuka with a grin.

As Daniel slipped into the shoes, the Guardian Buffalo asked if he was hungry, and Daniel responded with a firm nod.

"Why don't you settle in with your fellow warriors. An attendant will bring you some food," said the Guardian Buffalo.

"Thank you," said Daniel but his eyes lit up as he also said *thank you* in Vietnamese with a smile, "*cảm ơn bạn!*"

The Guardian Buffalo smirked and remarked, "You've been practicing."

Daniel looked proud and replied happily, "I have!" He then walked toward Clara and Yuka.

They waved back and he smiled as he settled into a cross legged position across from them.

"Your hair is all damp," Yuka remarked.

"I just finished swimming and took another shower when I got home. I have a swim meet next week… by the way, did you know we were only gone for like thirty minutes?" asked Daniel.

Clara and Yuka smiled and answered that they did just as a buffalo attendant placed a tray of food in front of Daniel. *"Cảm ơn bạn!"* he responded in Vietnamese for *thank you* along with a slight nod.

"Oh wow, *bánh mì*!" Daniel exclaimed excitedly!

"What's a *bánh mì*?" asked Yuka.

"It's a Vietnamese sandwich. Usually there is, you know, what we don't eat here on Azen, in it, but this smells so good. Here, try some," said Daniel as he crushed the crusty bread as he broke off a couple of pieces, which he gave to Yuka and Clara.

Their eyes lit up as they chewed through the soft warm baguette to find a fresh taste of pickled vegetables and grilled tofu. With their seeming approval, Daniel voraciously tore into the *bánh mì* himself and his eyes rolled back as his tastebuds took in its freshness.

"Who would have thought that the best vegetarian *bánh mì* would be made by Vietnamese water buffalos!" said Daniel as Clara and Yuka laughed.

"Please, try some of our food too," said Clara invitingly as she and Yuka used the other ends of their chopsticks to place a dumpling and a piece of *tamago* omelet onto his plate.

"Yum! Thanks!" said Daniel appreciatively. "Are we just waiting for Sung?"

Both Clara and Yuka nodded.

"I wonder how he did on his chem test?" Daniel wondered aloud. "Did you wait long for me?"

"About an hour," said Yuka. "I was here first. Well, after Clara."

Daniel looked at Clara and asked, "Why are we here? It's a little sooner than I thought."

Clara demurred a bit and looked up into the staring eyes of Daniel and Yuka. "It's a mission and if I don't succeed, the Panda Kingdom could be in danger."

There was silence as Daniel looked at Yuka and she turned to Clara, "What kind of danger?"

"Let's wait for Sung. The Guardian Panda will explain everything," asked Clara.

Daniel and Yuka assented to Clara's wishes and continued to talk as they finished up their lunches. Their conversations revolved around their realization that they had only been gone for so little time when they returned home, about how they continued manifesting their Qi elemental powers, and how they peppered their mothers to teach them more of their own languages.

The afternoon soon turned into early evening and Sung still had not materialized. The three warriors were beginning to wonder what had happened to him, but they were assured by the guardians that all was fine. They were told that sometimes, it may take hours or a day before a warrior materialized. But just as the sun started to dip toward the horizon, and the Guardian Tiger suggested that everyone return to their respective quarters, the water Wu Portal Book became aglow in a warm light. Its glow was even more spectacular in the waning light as Sung materialized out of thin air.

"Wow, that is so cool!" said Daniel, seeing for the first time how a warrior materialized from the Portal Book.

"Welcome back, Emperor Warrior Kim," said the Guardian Tiger as he straightened up.

Sung placed his hands on the sides of the stone tablet and turned into the Guardian Tiger's voice as his eyes lit up.

"*Annyeonghaseyo!* Guardian Tiger! It so good to see you again!" exclaimed Sung.

Sung heard someone yell "Fire!" He turned around to see Daniel waving at him, along with Clara and Yuka. "Ice!" Sung yelled back but before Sung could walk off, a tiger attendant brought him a pair of shoes.

As Sung slipped into the shoes, Clara admired his slender frame in a pair of navy-blue sweats and a black T-shirt. *He was looking quite athletic*, she thought.

Sung acknowledged the other three guardians and hustled over to the group. He fist bumped Daniel and waved gently to Clara and Yuka.

"You're last," said Clara teasingly.

"Oh, man. Am I really? I was playing StarCraft," said Sung before Daniel interjected, "Protoss?"

Sung gave Daniel an approving look and said, "Is there any other way?"

Yuka leaned into Clara and whispered, "What are they talking about?"

"Boy stuff," said Clara with a playful eyeroll.

The young warriors were about to excitedly talk to one another when the Guardian Panda interrupted them. "Empress and emperor warriors, as we now have all of you and that it is just about dinner time, let's walk down to the meal table."

The warriors nodded, and before they walked down to the meal table, attendants brought Sung, Yuka, and Daniel their respective weapons. They held onto their weapons fondly as they welcomed being reunited with them. At the meal table, they smiled with a sense of familiarity as they took their regular seats. As the guardians took their seats, cooks from each kingdom brought forth a selection of dishes: Chinese dumplings and *baos*; Korean rice cakes, kimchi pancakes and tofu *chigae*; Japanese *tamago* based dishes, and Vietnamese spring rolls and vegetable crepes. Though eager to dive into the food, each of the warrior waited respectfully until the Guardian Panda said, "Please enjoy your dinner."

Each warrior savored the dishes that they were so familiar with. They enjoyed dining family style, which let them share each other's Azen Asian cuisine. The style of the foods echoed what they had at home, but the flavors were so distinctly enhanced that they allowed them to taste everything anew. As they were close to finishing the food, the Guardian Panda gathered everyone's attention.

"Empress and emperor warriors," started the Guardian Panda. "On behalf of the guardians and the all the kingdom leaders, we are delighted that you are back on Azen. You must be wondering why we have called you back here. As you know, the Bamboo Jade was shattered in the battle with the first Warlock army. Despite the hopelessness that we first felt, somehow, Empress Warrior Wu awoke the hidden power of her own earthen jade bracelet. We do not know how this was possible, but the impossible did happen. However, after further investigation, we have determined that the jade bracelet has micro-fractures that makes its power temporary."

"What happens now?" asked Daniel.

"He's getting to that," said Clara.

"In order to find another suitable jade that will endure the test of time here on Azen, Empress Warrior Wu will need to search for one, in the Forbidden Cave of Jade Mountain," said the Guardian Panda ominously.

Silence befell the warriors as the Guardian Panda continued, "We, the inhabitants of Azen do not know much about the jade's powers. It is something only that the warriors may wield and now, it seems, only a warrior may discover once more."

The Guardian Panda recounted the entire historical discovery of the jade bestowed on each animal kingdom by its empress or emperor warrior. How the jade's intrinsic power to enhance the battle armor was refined over hundreds of years. How the jade's discovery was critical for turning the tide of battle against the Warlock. And how finally, after a thousand years, one of the jades finally shattered, and finding its replacement was essential for the ongoing battle against the Warlock.

Yuka, Daniel, and Sung were held spellbound by the story of the jade's origin. The burden of responsibility was already upon their shoulders, and now the search for a new Bamboo Jade was critical to winning against future Warlock battles.

"So, what is the next step?" asked Sung cautiously.

"I need to go into the Forbidden Cave and search for the one jade to command all the green jades," said Clara solemnly.

"Whoa. And only warriors can go in because all past kingdom animals who went in never came back out?" asked Sung inquisitively.

"It seems so," said Clara when Daniel blurted out, "The four of us in the Forbidden Cave?"

"Actually, no," interjected the Guardian Panda. "We need to be mindful to protect you at all costs. As Empress Warrior Satoh wields the only jade for our winged forces, she will stay. Empress Warrior Wu and myself have discussed it, and she will choose between the two emperor warriors to accompany her on her search."

The Guardian Panda looked down at Clara and asked, "Empress Warrior Wu, who shall it be?"

Clara suddenly felt all eyes fall onto her. She'd never felt so nervous about making a decision. She looked at Sung, who looked back at her blankly, while Daniel looked at her anxiously. She quickly looked down. She didn't want to put anyone in danger, but if she was being honest with herself, she was scared. She didn't want to be alone in the dreaded Forbidden Cave, especially when she didn't know what to expect. She looked back up and uttered, "I choose Sung."

Sung nodded in silence until Daniel broke the tense silence. "Why did you choose Sung?

Clara was taken aback by the question and she responded, "I don't know, he…"

"It's because I'm half, right?" said Daniel agitatedly.

"No, it's not that…"

"Don't lie! You feel that I may not be able to measure up," yelled Daniel as he started up.

Sung got up and said, "Hey, that's not fair. She's our fellow warrior…"

Daniel beamed frustratingly at Sung and stammered, "You're lucky! No one has ever thought you were less because you are half!"

The mighty water buffalo rose from his seat and towered over Daniel as he looked up, "Emperor Warrior Nguyen, this tone is unnecessary. Empress Warrior Wu has chosen, and we must respect her decision."

Daniel sat in mute frustration as he brooded over what had just transpired.

"Daniel," said Clara soothingly. "Please believe me when I tell you that I don't think any less of you."

Daniel stayed silent, then backed away from the table, "Of course you would say that. All my life, I've been told that I was only half. I need to get away. Guardian Buffalo, I'm sorry," said Daniel as he walked away.

Before the Guardian Buffalo could stop him, Daniel invoked the thrust Qi element and flew off into the night sky, leaving only the three warriors to realize that their fourth warrior may have just abandoned them.

NINE

The next morning at the Portal Circle, Clara, Yuka, and Sung milled about as they reflected on the tense night that had just passed. A bit of wind had been taken from their sails, and their team felt incomplete. Everyone was in their training attire, their respective colors marking the top edging of their training tops along the right shoulder line.

"Has anyone heard from Daniel this morning?" asked Sung as he readjusted the outward flap, which magnetically snapped into place.

"No," said Clara glumly. "Guardian Panda told me not to pursue it, and that the Guardian Buffalo would handle it."

"Same," said Yuka as she looked up to see the Guardian Panda, Tiger, and Crane talking in hushed tones outside of the Portal Circle. She looked down at her moon star and felt all the more powerful with it at her waist.

Clara's eyes looked up as the sound of hooves clattered onto the stone Portal Circle. It was the Guardian Buffalo, and by his side was Daniel, with the Club Horn of *Kting Voar*. Soon everyone's attention focused on the Guardian Buffalo and Daniel as they approached the middle of the Portal Circle.

"Good morning, Guardian Buffalo and Emperor Warrior Nguyen," said the Guardian Panda cautiously as he and the other guardians walked into the Portal Circle.

"Good morning, fellow guardians and emperor and empress warriors," said the Guardian Buffalo. "Emperor Warrior Nguyen has something he'd like to say this morning."

Daniel turned to see the Guardian Buffalo's stern eye on him, and he timidly took a couple of steps toward his fellow warriors.

With a loud exhale, he began to speak. "I'm sorry. I was a real jerk yesterday. I didn't mean what I said. All my life, I felt ashamed of my Vietnamese side, and since coming to Azen, it's the first time I finally saw how important it was to me. And when I'm among you, I feel I can be, you know, Asian with you guys. And yesterday, when Clara chose Sung instead, all that rejection that I held onto just came back, and I felt I was being left out because my Vietnamese side wasn't enough. But I know now that wasn't it, and I was just… scared. And for that I'm sorry," Daniel said sincerely as his voice trailed off.

Clara, Yuka, and Sung rushed up to Daniel to comfort him, as Sung was the first to say, "Bro man, you know we don't feel that way about you." Daniel looked up and nodded sheepishly.

Yuka came up to his side, "You're one of us, we're part of a team," she said comfortingly.

"We're the Azen Warriors," said Clara with a smile.

Daniel looked up at Clara, nodded and muttered under this breath, "For the first time, I found where my Asian side belonged, and I was scared that you weren't going to accept it. But I know now that it was me and not you. That's the truth."

Clara's eyes glistened and repeated Daniel's last word, "Truth."

"Do you feel better now, Emperor Warrior Nguyen?" asked the Guardian Buffalo.

Daniel wiped away a tear and nodded.

"Good. Let's all return to our Portal Books and allow the Guardian Panda to explain what's ahead," said the Guardian Buffalo.

With everyone back in their places and composed, the Guardian Panda summoned forth from the earth Wu Portal Book a fiery stream that wove itself into an outline of a mountain.

"This is Jade Mountain," said the Guardian Panda as he pointed to a large cave entrance at the base. "This is where we mine the illumination jades that give us light. It was all we ever found at first. But once the past Panda Emperor Warrior discovered the first green jade and showed our pandas where to mine for more, we've been mining it since. The other warriors were able to find the other jades, and as I mentioned, harnessing the power of these jades turned the tide of battle in our favor."

"During the peacetime between lunar cycles, animals from all the kingdoms mine for jade and protect it. Jade Mountain is large, and we don't believe we have even come close to finding all the jade hidden within the mountain itself, even after a thousand years of mining. But during the battle cycle, only the summoned kingdoms actively mine the mountain. Due to the strategic importance of the mountain, the Dragon Kingdom provides a dedicated sentinel to guard the mountain."

"There are dragons on Azen?" asked Clara excitedly as her eyes bulged.

"Yes, there are," said the Guardian Panda. "They are wise, benevolent, and powerful creatures, and they are aligned to the Wu metal element. But unlike the populations of the other kingdoms that are in the thousands, they are only in the hundreds."

The Guardian Panda wove another fiery image that enveloped the warriors and took them through the cave and its complex systems of tunnels and shafts. The Guardian Panda pointed to a long and solitary tunnel that ended in a cave entrance inside the mountain. Beyond the cave entrance was nothing more than an unknown dark mist.

"This is the cave entrance from which no Azen creature has ever returned. Thousands of years ago, miners discovered this natural tunnel that opened up into a cavern. The only thing that they found in this cavern was this odd cave entrance. The Portal Book usually reveals what we may have seen, but as no creature has ever returned, the Portal Book cannot reveal anything beyond this cave entrance. Even with the return of the original five warriors, who have the distinction of being called the Jade Warriors, their experience in the cave is shrouded in mystery. The only thing that we can gather is that one of the Jade Warriors let slip that beyond the cave entrance was a labyrinth. Though we don't know too much, we do know that it yielded the jades that commands all other like jades. All the jades reinforce our battle armor, but they also impart slightly different powers for each warrior. Empress Warrior Satoh's white jade has the power of replication. Empress Warrior Wu's green jade has the power of accuracy. Emperor Warrior Kim's blue jade has the power of resonance. Lastly, Emperor Warrior Nguyen's red jade has the power to amplify its force.

"After the mysterious disappearance of the reclusive order of the Azen monks long ago, the cave entrance was sealed off by Azen decree of the Kingdom Council and is guarded at all times. This will be the first time this cave will be unsealed in over a millennium. The Panderess has already made the request of the Kingdom Council, and they have approved it for this vital mission of retrieving a new green jade."

"There is no advice that I or anyone else can provide. It would seem that only warriors can enter the cave, retrieve the jade, and come out unscathed. So, Empress Warrior Wu and Emperor Warrior Kim, are you two ready to embark on this mission?"

Clara raised her hand. The Guardian Panda nodded, and she asked, "What was it that Emperor Warrior Hong said again? To 'remain true?'"

"Yes, that is all that he said," replied the Guardian Panda.

"Then, if Sung doesn't mind, I'd like to change my decision about who I'd like to go into the cave with. I want Daniel to come with me," said Clara firmly.

"Hey, you don't need to do this, Clara," said Daniel. "I'm okay with you taking Sung, really I am."

"No Daniel, I'd like for you to go with me," said Clara. "Besides, we're going into some dark cave, and you control fire, so you can light our way."

"She's got a point," said Sung. "It's her decision."

Daniel looked over to Sung and then back to Clara, "Then I'll go with you."

"Excellent, it's settled then," interjected the Guardian Panda. "Guardian Crane, would you mind calling forth the squadron?"

The Guardian Crane nodded and emitted a couple of quick squawks. Five additional cranes and one eagle rose over the boulders surrounding the Portal Circle. A pair of feathered aviators landed by each of the Portal Books. A kingdom attendant also came up alongside each of the Portal Books with a cloth bundle.

"Warriors, the flight to Jade Mountain may be cold," said the Guardian Crane. "So we have provided you these robes."

Clara, Sung, Yuka, and Daniel walked back to their Portal Books with curiosity. As Clara got closer, the panda attendant unfurled a rich green robe with white edging along the front. On the left side, along the upper chest, was an embroidered panda head. It was beautiful and as she approached, another attendant beckoned for her bow and quiver. With a turn, she eased her arms into the robe as the attendant draped it over her shoulders. As Clara brought her hands to the front, the front white edging on each side of the entire length of the robe magically snapped together. She looked up awestruck at the Guardian Panda.

"It's magnetic," said the Guardian Panda.

"Oh cool!" said Clara and she looked up at everyone else. Sung had a rich blue robe, Yuka wore a white robe, while Daniel was playfully pulling apart the magnetic front edging of his red robe and watching them snap back together.

"Must they always play with the robes?" asked the Guardian Tiger of the Guardian Panda, who smirked back.

"Warriors, please harness in and let's head to Jade Mountain," commanded the Guardian Panda.

Sung wrapped the harness around his waist and clipped in as Daniel got his attention. He looked up to his right, and Daniel said, "Thanks, bro." Sung smiled and gave him an air fist bump and gently petted the crane's nape and said, "Ready."

When everyone had signaled to their respective feathered aviator that they were harnessed in, the Guardian Crane, with Yuka aboard her, flapped her great wings and soared upward. All the other cranes and one eagle flew upward and formed a V formation headed toward Jade Mountain.

TEN

Though she could have flown to Jade Mountain on her own power, Yuka enjoyed riding atop her Guardian Crane. With her mighty wings, she was master of the air, flying effortlessly through skies over terrain that she knew all too well. The wind ruffled through the top layer of the Guardian Crane's sturdy feathers and whisked through Yuka's hair. She needed a better way to tie it back during flight, she thought, but that was a small penance for the freedom she felt as she soared through the air.

Yuka looked to her right and saw Clara, Sung, and Daniel in formation. They looked equally calm and were enjoying the flight. Her head twisted to the left, and she saw the Guardian Panda, Tiger, and Buffalo also in formation. She smiled as the Guardian Tiger looked to be taking a cat nap on the back of his crane.

"We're almost there, Empress Warrior Satoh," said the Guardian Crane.

"Mmmm… okay," replied Yuka.

Yuka peered over the Guardian Crane's shoulder as the smattering of cloud cover soon gave way to a large and eerily jagged mountain ahead. *That's Jade Mountain,* she said to herself.

A squawk from the Guardian Crane signaled the squadron to follow her as she began her descent. As she continued to look over the Guardian Crane's shoulder, Yuka could see that the entire mountain was surrounded by a formidable bamboo wall. At regular intervals were similar *tō* towers that acted as watch towers, and for a moment, a shudder went down Yuka's spine. She could see that the top three floors of each tower were open, and several cranes were on watch. On the lower level, she saw mechanized crossbows manned by pandas. The Guardian Panda was right: Jade Mountain was highly guarded.

She felt the Guardian Crane bank right and head toward a large open area behind the bamboo wall. The winged aviators soon opened their great wings as they descended. With grace and surefootedness, all the cranes and one eagle landed.

"Empress and emperor warriors, welcome to Jade Mountain," declared the Guardian Crane. "Please climb off carefully, and we'll head straight to the

Forbidden Cave."

When the warriors landed on their feet, straightened up, and adjusted their weapons along their new robes, they noticed a flurry of activity. Mighty buffalos were pushing rugged bamboo carts that contained large chunks of rock on metal wheels along metal tracks. In one cart, the broken rocks glistened green. It was jade.

As the guardians and warriors got closer to the mountain entrance, many of the miners briefly stopped what they were doing and bowed to the guardians, but it took a moment longer for them to take in the emperor and empress warriors who were visiting them.

"Don't mind them, emperor and empress warriors," said the Guardian Buffalo. "It's not often that they get to see any, and definitely not all, the emperor and empress warriors at one time."

Clara eyed the five sets of rails running parallel to each other along the ground when a large shadow slithered across the ground. Someone let out an excited outburst. She looked upward toward the sky and saw in the air the long, large body of something slithering through the air. Its four clawed feet were tucked neatly along its scaly body, and the hair from its head flared backwards.

It was a dragon.

"That is U-Yong," said the Guardian Panda. "He's a wise one."

"You've talked with him?" asked Clara with amazement as she watched U-Yong disappear somewhere atop the mountain.

"Oh yes, he's flown down from time to time," answered the Guardian Panda. "Come, we need to get to the Forbidden Cave."

Clara followed along with her warriors until they came upon the large, arched mountain entrance. The outer rim was carved smooth into a semi-circle, but the keystone was the most prominent. It was embedded with several oblong jades of varying colors.

As they passed into the mountain tunnel, Clara could see that the sides were chiseled smooth. There were reinforcing bamboo arches along the entire length of the tunnel. Above was an orderly arrangement of large illumination jades that gave light to what would have been eerie darkness.

As they walked, they saw several tunnel entrances to the left, and buffalos were pushing the same type of rugged bamboo carts in and out. From deep within the tunnels rang the unmistakable dull, repetitive clanging of miners working deep within the mountain.

They moved past the mine tunnels and followed a solitary tunnel before they entered a larger cavern. Here they heard no work noise, and the warriors continued following their guardians.

Clara looked up and saw ahead of her what looked like an arch-shaped stone set into the wall of the rocky cave. A group of battle pandas, tigers, and buffalos was lined up in front of it.

As the guardians approached, a battle panda in full armor stepped out of the formation and bowed toward the group. The entire group of guardians and warriors did the same.

Clara looked past the Guardian Crane and peered at the stone embedded in the asymmetrical arched cave opening. The opening wasn't much bigger than the Guardian Panda. Along the entire rim of the cave entrance were carvings in several Asian languages. Her eyes followed along the carvings until she came to the Chinese carving. It read ominously, *"Danger."*

"Guardians, emperor and empress warriors," the battle panda stated. "I'm the Protector Captain of the Forbidden Cave of Jade Mountain. I received your message yesterday from the Kingdom Council, and we are ready. Do you have the four keys?"

The Guardian Panda stepped forward and produced a two-foot-long smooth metal rod that had grooves along its length.

"Thank you for preparing for our arrival," said the Guardian Panda as he handed over the key to a panda attendant that took it.

"It is my duty," said the Protector Captain as the Guardian Tiger handed over a similar metal rod, which was taken by another panda attendant.

The Guardian Buffalo then handed over his key and finally, the Guardian Crane, with her key in her beak, handed it over to another panda attendant.

"What's going on?" whispered Clara to the Guardian Panda.

"The stone slab is held in place by an intricate locking system. It takes four keys to open it, and each animal kingdom has one key. As the keys are pushed further into the keyhole of the stone slab, it retracts several metal latches that lock into the side of the cave itself. Only the immediate opening of the cave could be carved out to receive the stone slab. The master mason who was commissioned to work on the slab became ill if he stayed within the cave entrance for too long. This slab has been in its place for over a thousand years and has not been breached since."

Daniel suddenly felt the need to grip the club horn a bit tighter. Everyone was silent as the panda attendants firmly inserted the four key rods. As each groove triggered the locking mechanism within, a mechanical sound emanated from it that echoed inside the cavern. When all four key rods were inserted about three quarters of the way, the panda attendants stepped aside.

Two large buffalos stepped toward the stone slab. They each carried a large, right-angled metal rod with a hook on the end. They inserted that end into an oblong hole in the center of the slab and turned the metal rods in opposing right angles to each other so that they were parallel to the ground. The buffalos walked behind the metal rods and in unison, dug their hooves into the ground, and pushed. At first the stone slab did not budge, but after a grunted push, the screeching of rock against rock tore through everyone's ears.

As they pushed, the full length of the stone slab revealed itself, and once it was free, they continued pushing until it was clear of the entrance.

A gust of stale air gushed out of the Forbidden Cave. It caused all the warriors to shudder for a moment as they felt something deathly in that air, which had been locked away for over a thousand years. Clara looked at her fellow warriors, who also looked at each other with consternation. They turned their stare toward the cave entrance, which was darkness itself.

"This is the Forbidden Cave," said the Guardian Panda. "The creatures of Azen are not meant to return from this cave once they enter it. We do not know why. But the five Jade Warriors all entered and successfully returned with the one jade that commands them all. We have to believe that you will also be successful. I can only advise you what was said by the Emperor Warrior Hong: 'Remain True.' Take it for what it is, and I wish I could tell you more. Are there any questions?"

"How long were the warriors gone for before they came back?" asked Daniel cautiously.

The Guardian Panda curiously looked at the Guardian Tiger and said, "For some warriors, it was only a matter of a few hours, but for one warrior, it was two days."

"Whoa! Two days?" said Clara anxiously.

"Yes, but it was only a few hours for him. But you are being provided with some food just in case," said the Guardian Panda as two battle pandas stepped forward with a sling pouch for Clara and Daniel. "Inside, you'll find some *baos*, water, and another pouch, which you can take out now."

Both Clara and Daniel fumbled with the clasp on the sling pouch before pulling out another pouch, whose contents rattled. Clara pulled apart the drawstring and her face was alit from the many illumination jade pebbles within it.

"What are these for?" asked Clara.

"We don't know what it's like in there, so you may drop these along your way. They will light your way back to the entrance," said the Guardian Panda.

"Ah, like breadcrumbs," said Clara who nodded in understanding.

"Hansel and Gretel," Daniel muttered under his breath as he cinched up the pouch containing the illumination jade pebbles.

The two panda attendants took Clara's and Daniel's robes. They were then handed a foot-long bamboo stalk with a slit on its side.

"What's this?" asked Daniel as he held the green bamboo, which had the thickness of a large leek.

"Twist it," said the Guardian Panda. "It is an illumination jade torch."

Clara's eyes lit up as she twisted it as light from an illumination jade shone through the slit. "Just like the one from the crafts shop, but bigger."

Daniel did as Clara did and twisted his illumination jade torch to allow the light to shine through.

"To light your way and give you perpetual light," said the Guardian Panda. "You may also slip off the outer bamboo casing and twist it onto the bottom, which will act as a handle. But you have the fire Wu warrior with you, who should be able to invoke light at any time."

"He better," said Clara teasingly as Daniel smiled and twisted his jade torch off.

"Very well," started the Guardian Panda. "Let's send you off."

The Guardian Panda led Clara and Daniel to the dark entrance of the Forbidden Cave, which seemed to become a wall of impregnable darkness a few feet in. Her eyes wandered along the rim of the cave, and she was mystified by its veil of darkness. She looked down at the jade bracelet on her left wrist and remembered that the one her mother gave to her was on the Bow of Destiny slung across her front. She exhaled and looked up at Daniel, who looked a bit nervous.

"It's like the jitters I get before each swim meet," said Daniel as he repositioned his grip on the illumination jade torch with one hand and the club horn in the other.

"I think you can put away your club horn," Clara suggested.

"I don't know, we don't know what's in the cave. For all we know, it could be a bear," responded Daniel.

"There are no bears," said the Guardian Panda sternly.

Daniel looked up and felt his face flush, "Oh, sorry, no offense."

"I just think that whatever is in the cave isn't meant to hurt us, and if there is something in there, we shouldn't give it a reason to think we are a danger," said Clara.

Daniel thought for a moment and nodded. He inserted the club horn into the sheath across his back and relaxed.

Clara smiled and she looked back at Yuka and Sung, who both wore worried expressions. "Don't worry, we're the Azen Warriors. We'll be fine, and I'll come back with the green jade."

"Be careful," said Yuka as Sung said, "Yah, watch each other in there, you two."

Daniel nodded in Sung's direction as he faced forward. "Ready?" he asked Clara.

Clara looked up as strands of his dark brown hair fell across his forehead. "Yes, ready," she said as she let out a breath.

"Ladies first," said Daniel teasingly.

"Oh nice," said Clara sarcastically. "Ready to go, Guardian Panda."

"Remember, 'Remain True,'" said the Guardian Panda as he stepped aside.

Clara and Daniel twisted open their jade torches. They exhaled, and with the jade torches held before them, they stepped through the cave entrance to the Forbidden Cave of Jade Mountain.

Yuka and Sung moved in to watch Clara and Daniel advance into the cave when suddenly, Yuka exclaimed, "They're gone!"

ELEVEN

"It's so dark," whispered Clara as she held the illumination jade torch ahead of her. "I can barely see what's in front of me. And the air, it smells so… old."

"Look at the walls," said Daniel in a vexed tone as he paused. His fingertips slowly glided along the flat wall. "This can't be natural; someone must have carved this tunnel."

With her hand on the wall as well, Clara observed how the light from the jade torch glistened in the tiny nooks of the tunnel's wall. She turned her head to the left from where they came and exclaimed, "Where's the entrance?"

Daniel spun around in a panic. He could no longer see the cave entrance. He abruptly took a couple of steps from where they stood until Clara grabbed his hand. "Don't leave me!"

Daniel collected himself as he felt Clara's clammy and trembling hand in his. He exhaled and whispered, "Sorry."

"We need to stick together," Clara urged as she gently squeezed his hand then let it go.

"Yeah, right," said Daniel. "Let's walk back to the cave entrance."

Clara watched his confused expression as the white light cast eerie, jagged shadows across his features and the misty darkness enshrouded the rest of his face and body. She nodded and they timidly retraced their steps until Clara said, "Wait, I see them, kind of."

Daniel also peered through the darkness. He could see a blurred outline of the cave entrance and the silhouettes of Sung and Yuka beyond it. Behind them, they could make out the faint outlines of the guardians or the guards. They weren't sure.

"We're okay!" shouted Daniel. But there was no reaction from their fellow warriors.

"Maybe they can't hear us," said Clara as she waved futilely in Sung's and Yuka's direction.

Daniel opened his pouch of illumination jade pebbles and brought out a handful.

"What are you doing?" asked Clara.

"I'm going to make an arrow. So, when we see this arrow, we'll know we're headed in the right direction to get out of here," said Daniel nervously.

"Good idea," said Clara as she turned her gaze toward the dark, daunting tunnel. She let out a breath and turned as Daniel straightened up. He was looking down, and she cast her eyes downward and saw an arrow glowing away from her. She looked up at him, met his gaze and nodded. Her hand slid upward to the bow's grip, and she looked down at the jade bracelet, which caught the light of the jade torch. With her brown eyes looking up at Daniel's, she said, "Let's find that green jade."

Together, they turned their back to the cave's entrance as it was slowly enveloped by tendrils of darkness. As they walked, they dropped an illumination jade pebble onto the ground. They walked slowly and deliberately down the mysterious tunnel. They wondered who had chiseled it out. As they shone the light upward, they saw the ceiling was about ten feet high and six feet wide. Yet it seemed to go forever into the darkness.

"It's dead quiet," said Daniel.

"Don't say 'dead,'" Clara said with annoyance.

Daniel nodded and winced, "Dumb me. I think I can hear your heartbeat if I listen hard enough."

"No, you can't," said Clara, but she knew that her heart was racing and didn't want Daniel to hear it.

They pressed onward, holding the jade torches in front of them, trying to pierce the darkness. The darkness was silent and thick, hiding its secrets.

Clara peered deeper and something whisked by her neck. She let out a gasp and jumped back against the wall, causing Daniel to do the same.

"What?" he asked frantically.

Clara's eyes darted back and forth as her body trembled, "You didn't feel that?"

"Feel what?" asked Daniel as he reached for the handle of the club horn while his eyes darted left and right.

"Something touched my neck really fast," said Clara as she regripped her bow as her breathing quickened.

"Are you sure? I didn't feel anything," said Daniel.

"Hold on," said Clara as she set her jade torch on the ground, leaning it against the cave wall. She unslung the Bow of Destiny, loaded an arrow, and released the glowing jade-tipped arrow into the darkness. The pluck of the drawstring reverberated throughout the tunnel as the arrow whisked into the darkness. They listened intently and didn't hear the arrow hitting anything. Clara and Daniel looked at each other as she asked, "How long is this tunnel?"

"I don't know, but I'm not taking any chances," said Daniel, reaching to remove the club horn from his back. But Clara placed her hand on his shoulder.

"No. Whatever is in here helped the past warriors, and they came out fine. I don't think we want to be a threat to whatever may be in here, if there is anything in here at all," she said calmly.

Daniel paused and released his grip when his eyes lit up. "Hey, let me try something."

Daniel walked in front of Clara and invoked a fireball Qi element. It erupted and raced down the tunnel in a brilliant mix of glowing blue flares. Daniel's and Clara's eyes widened as they followed the burning bluish fireball down the seemingly infinite tunnel until it disappeared.

"Did you see that?" asked a stunned Daniel.

"Yah," said Clara. "What the hell? Why was it blue?"

"Beats me," said Daniel. "But it looks like we have a ways to go."

Clara nodded with trepidation and said, "Let's go."

They continued to walk cautiously until something caught their eyes up ahead.

"Hey, it's your arrow!" said Daniel. He quickened his pace as Clara followed.

"It's a corner," said Clara as she extended the jade torch to her left. Daniel walked into the corner, looked down another dark tunnel, and motioned with his eyes to Clara, who stepped in front of him. He reached up for the arrow, but Clara interjected, "Leave it, we can use it as a marker to help us find our way out."

Daniel nodded, and he followed Clara down yet another dark tunnel. It wasn't long before it bent to the right, then left, and another right. They suddenly stopped as a ramp appeared before them that led to a landing. They looked at each other and carefully climbed the ramp with their jade torches in front of them. As they neared the top, Daniel paused and peered over the ledge.

"What do you see?" whispered Clara.

"It's another tunnel," said Daniel as he stepped onto the landing. He turned around and extended his hand to Clara, which she took as he gently pulled her upward. When she straightened up, she shone her jade's light down the tunnel. Nothing revealed itself for more than ten feet or so. "Shall we?" asked Daniel as he dropped another illumination jade pebble. Clara nodded as they proceeded into the tunnel.

"I wonder who created these tunnels?" whispered Clara.

"Whoever they were, they were really skilled. These tunnels are perfectly square," said Daniel.

"Hey," exclaimed Clara. "What is that?"

Daniel looked at Clara's bowed head and saw white wisps swirling past his feet. He moved the jade's light and saw that the white wisps were coming from up ahead.

"Fog?" asked Clara?

"I think so?" said a bewildered Daniel.

"Oh my god, what's up ahead?" asked Clara nervously.

"Not sure, but we've come this far, we should see," said Daniel.

"Okay, but slowly," said Clara. "I'm starting to get a bad feeling."

Daniel gulped and said, "Yeah, me too."

They inhaled the stale air and exhaled as they moved into the tunnel's darkness. The wispy fog thickened and floated past their thighs. There was a touch of iciness each time it glanced their legs. They walked for what seemed like a hundred feet when the tunnel came to an abrupt end.

"It's a dead end," said Daniel as he placed his palm on the cool rocky wall in front of him.

"Can you please not say 'dead'?" pleaded Clara.

"Sorry."

"Let's go back?" asked Clara. "Maybe we missed a turn?"

"I don't think so," said Daniel. "But might as well."

Clara looked up at Daniel's blank expression and turned back the way they came. They had not walked more than fifty feet when Clara exclaimed, "What the hell?"

"What?" said Daniel as he came up behind her and he saw her hand on the wall.

"Where's the tunnel?!" yelled out Clara.

Before Daniel could respond, dark tendrils had seeped out from the walls' sides, and he yanked Clara's hand away as the tendrils met in the middle, solidifying into a new rock wall.

"What's happening?!" Clara yelled as she shone her jade torch from side-to-side as new dark tendrils drifted out, solidifying into new wall.

"The wall! It's growing," said Daniel frantically.

"But how?" asked Clara, stepping backwards as the dark misty tendrils were slithering out faster.

"Come on!" screamed Daniel. "We gotta go!"

"But it's a dead end down there too!" said Clara as she raced after Daniel, with only his shaky jade torch for her to follow.

Daniel slammed up against the dead end as his right palm frantically felt about the wall. Clara, wide eyed, also felt about the wall. It was solid, and although she didn't hear anything before, she now heard a distinct *click* whenever the dark tendrils solidified, and the clicks were quickening. She glanced down at the growing wall and she saw it: The wall was moving in on them. Her heart raced. *She was going to be slowly crushed by a wall formed by dark tendrils,* she thought. She heard the muffled sounds of Daniel futilely slapping on the wall behind her as tendrils continued to seep out of the wall and solidify—when suddenly, her right hand passed through the side of the wall.

She looked down, dumbfounded, and saw her hand had miraculously pushed through the rock wall as it disintegrated before her eyes. She frantically yelled out, "Here!"

Daniel looked down to see the seemingly solid wall around her hand dissolve away. He pivoted and glanced at the wall that was advancing towards them. Then suddenly, he too felt his hands dissolving the wall in front of them. It was a strange sensation to feel more of the wall dissolve under his hand. Clara looked up at him.

"Just push through!" screamed Clara.

Daniel nodded and pushed through the misty wall, which dissolved away into a new tunnel, with Clara at his side. Clara found it strange that in one instant, she could feel the solid wall but in the next, it dissolved away. They were barely ten feet into the new tunnel when they felt the entrance solidify behind them.

The silence was eerie. Clara and Daniel could swear they heard each other's heartbeats. They cautiously turned their jade torches towards the new wall behind them. It was still. They both let out a breath, but the momentary feeling of safety ended as new dark, misty tendrils slithered out, forming new wall.

Clara looked at Daniel with bulging eyes. "Push!" she yelled.

Daniel nodded, and he and Clara ran up against the tunnel's end and pushed through the dissolving rock until they came to another dead end. But Daniel found another part of the wall on the left that dissolved away, and Clara pushed through with him. They pushed through another twenty feet, their ears picking up the chilling clicking sounds behind them. Their palms came upon another dead end. The clicking was getting louder.

Daniel frantically felt around the right side of the wall while Clara felt around on the left. Suddenly, both of their hands dissolved the rock and they pushed through. They were not more than two feet in when a new wall rose between them as they turned to scream out to each other.

"Daniel!" screamed Clara as she shone her jade torch on the new wall separating her from Daniel. Her heart sank as she threw herself up against it. Her face crumbled when she looked about the small tunnel that she was in. Not more two feet deep, ten feet high and three feet wide. She was entombed.

"No!" Clara screamed out. "Daniel!"

But as she pressed her back against the new wall, it dissolved, and she glanced back. She took a few timid steps backwards as the new tunnel gave way. As the tunnel deepened by a few more feet, she looked toward the wall that sealed her off and said, "I'll find you Daniel."

Clara swept her jade torch along the edge of the opening and pushed through the face of the wall with her hand, deepening the tunnel. She heard nothing. The silence was thick, but she was thankful not to hear the dreaded clicking behind her. The wall continued to dissolve away, and after about fifty feet, Clara stopped. She turned around and she panicked, running back the way she came. Perhaps she could dissolve the wall away and reconnect with Daniel. She hoped that he was all right and that he had not been eaten by the wall. But soon, her frantic concern turned to confusion when she felt like she had run a hundred feet. *It can't be this long*, she thought.

She stopped in her tracks and ran the other way, certain she'd come to the end of the new wall—but the tunnel was endless. She stopped in utter confusion. She suddenly ran back toward where she thought she had separated from Daniel, but no end appeared. In confusion, she spun around in the tunnel, shining her jade torch all around when suddenly, she couldn't tell which end was which anymore.

She reached into her pouch, pulled out an illumination jade pebble, and dropped it on the ground. The jade's light glowed as it illuminated swirling white wisps on the ground that she hadn't noticed before. Her head turned in the direction that she believed she was separated from Daniel. As she walked some distance, her eyes caught something glowing on the ground. As she came closer, she looked down and stared in confusion at an illumination jade pebble.

"This can't be," said Clara as she looked left and right. She pulled out a few more jade pebbles and arranged them in the shape of an arrow facing what she thought was the tunnel entrance. She got up and looked toward the direction of the arrow and followed it. She looked back and could make out the faint glow of the jade pebbles. She turned her back on them and jogged down the tunnel when she suddenly saw it: her arrow of jade pebbles. *Was she going around in a circle?* she asked herself.

"Daniel!" she hollered out, her voice tinged with desperation. The darkness held steady and did not carry a response. More darkness crept in, leaving Clara all alone as she pressed herself up against the wall. She shone the jade's light to her left and then to her right as she choked back the tremors at the back of her throat. She reached up along the bow's grip and felt the jade bracelet under her hand and looked down at it. As the jade torch's light lit up the bracelet's dark green jade, it almost seemed to absorb the jade's white light. She reached up and gently swiped the curve of the bracelet with her left index finger and its familiarity brought some comfort. She sniffled a couple of times and whimpered, "Mom, Baba, help."

TWELVE

"Clara!" screamed Daniel desperately as he pounded on the newly created rock that sealed him into the small rocky alcove. It only took a moment for the growing rock to separate him from Clara. He realized that this had been the goal of the labyrinth from the very beginning. If he couldn't go back from where he came from, then he would go where the dissolved rock led him. But he hadn't gone more than fifty feet when guilt ate at him, and he ran back to where he was separated from Clara. After futilely pounding on the rock, he went back toward the other end and continued frenetically dissolving the rock ahead of him.

"Damn it," said Daniel as he pounded the hard cool rock in front of him. Yet another dead end. *I must have missed a turn off,* he thought as he carefully doubled back, feeling the side of the wall against his palm, hoping it would dissolve. He had moved what he thought was fifty feet when he felt nothing but solid rock. Frustration set in as he looked left and right and saw only darkness.

Daniel ran his fingers roughly through his dark brown hair and pressed his hand against the back of his neck in frustration, trying to collect his thoughts. In an instant, he flung his fingers down the direction of the tunnel from which he came from and invoked the fireball Qi element. Like before, a glowing blue fireball flared out and raced down the tunnel only to disappear. He flung his arm toward the other end and invoked another bluish fireball, watching it fly off. But this time, it didn't disappear into the darkness. It illuminated an outline of an entrance and flew upward.

Daniel's eyes lit up as he ran in that direction. With his heart pounding, he raced down the tunnel with his jade torch in hand. The illuminated darkness gave way until finally, a faint outline of the tunnel's end came into view. Daniel's eyes lit up as he raced ahead until finally, he burst into a square chamber. He quickly scanned the room and saw that each of its walls had an entrance in its center. In the middle of the chamber was a small circular pool of water surrounded by a stone wall. He shone the jade's light upward and saw that the walls flared outward. At regular intervals, ledges were carved into the rocky walls. The walls rose for as far as the jade's light allowed. He suddenly felt immensely small.

As he approached the mysterious pool of water, he saw it was very still and dark. His vexed reflection stared back at him along with the glow of the jade torch. He leveled his eyes on the three other entrances. He chose the center one and cautiously walked through it. As he extended the jade torch outward, two bluish eyes suddenly stared back at him. He gulped as he slowly backed out from the entrance. The large blue eyes moved toward him. Soon, the rest of the creature's body started to luminesce in a similar blue glow.

As Daniel stepped out of the tunnel entrance and clumsily walked backwards around the pool of water, the creature slowly exited the tunnel, first its large snout, then its massive shoulders eased along with its hooved muscular legs. Soon, its entire massive body emerged, but its most impressive feature were its horns, aglow in a bluish tint.

It was a water buffalo.

Daniel's eyes bulged, darting from left to right as a water buffalo entered the room from those entrances. Their blue glow illuminated the chamber. The water buffalos were large, a bit larger than his Guardian Buffalo, and their presence was daunting. The three buffalos looked at him with firm eyes and soul-piercing stares.

Daniel shone the jade torch's light at each of the buffalos. They were unfazed. With the jade light on the center buffalo, he looked back into its gaze, which seemed to pierce right through him. He wanted to believe the ethereal blue water buffalos before him were not a danger. He slowly straightened up with the jade torch in his hand. He bowed to the buffalo in the center and then to each of the other buffalos.

The three buffalos bowed back and looked back at Daniel.

"I'm Daniel," he said with a nervous tone.

There was no response from the buffalos, and he continued, "Do you speak English?" His face dropped embarrassingly at his gaffe as his hands went to shield his eyes momentarily. *What a stupid thing to ask,* he thought.

The buffalo in the center tamped its hoof thrice and the white wisps on the ground suddenly wrapped themselves around Daniel's legs. He jumped in panic until the center buffalo shook his head sternly and stared back at Daniel. He stilled his jittery movements and nervously allowed the white wisps to work its way up his torso. As they reached his face, he jolted his head back as the white wisps entered his nostrils. His hands began to tremble, and his breathing raced as he felt the wisps swirling in his head like noodles and suddenly, the wisps retreated and untwined themselves from his body.

"*What do you call yourself?*" a voice asked in Vietnamese.

"Whoa, who said that?" said a startled Daniel as he looked at each of the water buffalos.

The buffalos were steadfast silent, and the Vietnamese voice came again, "*What do you call yourself?*"

It was in his head, Daniel realized. Somehow, the white wisps allowed the buffalos to talk to him in his mind. Daniel straightened up and said, "Daniel Nguyen Parker."

The buffalos did not flinch, and the voice came again, "*What do you call yourself?*"

Daniel nodded and realized what he needed to say. In Vietnamese he said, "*I am Emperor Warrior Nguyen.*"

The buffalo on the right looked at Daniel up and down and turned to the center buffalo. "*He is different,*" he said in Vietnamese.

The water buffalo on the left looked at Daniel with the same curiosity as he inhaled Daniel's scent. "*There is another,*" he said firmly.

Sensing that the water buffalos detected it as he had gotten it all his life, Daniel said begrudgingly, "*I'm half Vietnamese.*"

The three water buffalos looked at Daniel quizzically and continued to stare until one spoke. "*Present the Club Horn of Kting Voar.*"

Daniel jolted at the request. He quickly leaned his jade torch against the low stone wall framing the pool of water. With his right hand, he reached back to grab the club horn's handle and brought it over his shoulder. He rested the top part of the horn on his left hand as he held it with his right hand. Even in the bluish luminescence, the red jade glistened as the three water buffalos fixed their eyes on it. They returned their gaze onto Daniel.

"*Are you true?*" a voice asked.

Daniel paused, not sure if he understood the question and cautiously uttered, "Yes?"

The water buffalos stared at him until the one in the center motioned him to come forward to the pool. Daniel shuffled forward, and he could see the buffalos' bristling fur along their body. Each hair tip was tinged with a bluish glow. He could faintly make out the bulging muscles that curved along each of their bodies. The buffalo on the left stomped on the ground beneath him, causing the water to ripple

Daniel's attention was diverted to the circular ripples in the dark pool, which intensified as a ghostly image started to appear: a living room. His living room, the way he remembered it when he was a child of five. Daniel let out a trembling gasp as the memory in his mind was crystal clear. The front door was visible, and to the right of it was a couch and a coffee table. The coffee table was strewn with a box of napkins, a TV remote, and a half-drunk bottle of water. On the floor were scattered toys, and he saw one of them angrily kicked against the door. A White man of medium stature came into the room, carrying a suitcase as he strode angrily toward the door. His arm was suddenly yanked by someone: his mother. She was frantically pulling on him, but he resisted. The angst on her face was evident as she tried to pull him back, but to no avail. Her petite size was no match for his bigger frame.

"Please! Don't go!" Daniel's mother pleaded when his father turned and violently pushed her away, breaking her hold on his arm. He beamed angrily at her and yelled back, "I didn't marry a *gook* to raise a *gook*!"

His father reached the doorknob and simply walked out, forever. His mother wailed, and the vantage point switched to that of his sobbing mother. Her face was buried in her hands and as she choked back her emotions, she caught five-year-old Daniel looking at her, confused. She brought her hands to her chest, calming herself before she got up. She steadily walked toward the open door and looked out before closing it. She wiped her tears, pressed down her dress, and turned around. With her face somewhat composed, she came toward Daniel and hugged him as the room gently swayed. He saw her mother's face with a forced smile. She looked at him and said, "You are not that bad word, you are Vietnamese. You are my adorable Vietnamese son."

Daniel's eyes welled up with tears. That scene had been scarred into his memory but seeing it so clearly in the water was too surreal for him.

"*Are you true?*" asked one of the buffalos.

Daniel looked up and he wrestled with the memory. He felt that his father abandoned him and his mother because he was part Vietnamese, and he had blamed himself for that. If he wasn't Vietnamese, his father would have stayed. But that would have meant that his mother wouldn't be

Vietnamese. He realized just then that it was his father's weakness that led to his cowardly decision to abandon his Vietnamese mother and him when he was only five. It was his Vietnamese mother's strength and resilience that nurtured and watched over him.

Daniel looked up at each of the buffalos and nodded. "Yes," he whispered.

The buffalo on the right tamped down on the ground as its dark eyes stared back into the water. Daniel looked back into the clear, dark water when another circular ripple emanated from the center as another image started to emerge.

He could see his mother's face as she struggled to carry home a brown paper bag of groceries. She was wearing a summer dress and slingback shoes. It was early evening, and the sun was just dipping, which brought welcome relief from the heat. She was minding her own business as a navy-blue car slowly came alongside her. She eyed it suspiciously and saw two men in the car. The windows were rolled down as a man with a closely shaved head on the passenger side rested his forearm atop the door. He was eyeing her lecherously, and this made the hair on the back on her neck stand up. She averted her gaze and picked up her pace as the man blurted out, "Hey honey, what's your name?"

She ignored him as she heard an ominous laugh from the car. The voice came again. "Come on, you sweet Asian thing, can't we be friends?"

She kept on walking and shifted the bag of groceries, which contained Vietnamese leafy vegetables, a fresh baguette, and her clear water bottle, to her left side. To her relief, the car behind the men honked its horn. Before it sped up, the rude men laughed as the car sped away.

She let out her breath and quickened her pace. Before she turned down the path to her townhouse, she looked about to make sure that the car was nowhere to be seen. She raced up the path and pressed the bag of groceries up against the wall as she leaned into it. With her head bowed, she choked back her fear and anger. Her deep breaths calmed as she wiped away the tears that welled between her eyelids. She took another deep breath, pulled away from the wall, inserted the key into the doorknob and opened it.

"*Mẹ!*" she heard as present-day Daniel called out to her. She stepped into the living room, placed the groceries down, and closed the door. With a turn, she smiled at Daniel as if nothing had happened.

The image slowly sunk into the depths of the pool.

Daniel looked up and he was livid. His hands were clenched tighter around the club horn as he witnessed, for the first time, his own mother being harassed and how she had hidden it from him. He had no idea that she was facing her own burdens of being Vietnamese while he was grappling with his, which he was too ambivalent and ashamed to share with her.

"*Mẹ!* I'm sorry!" exclaimed Daniel as his vision was blurred by tears. "I didn't know you had to put up with it too!"

"*Are you true?*" asked one of the buffalos in Vietnamese.

Daniel wiped away his tears and nodded his head fervently. "Yes," was all he could say between his emotions of anger, frustration, and admiration for his mother.

The center water buffalo stomped on the ground with his right hoof, and Daniel, already feeling drained, looked back into the still water. A ripple emanated from the center once more, and a ghostly image started to appear, and he saw strangely, another pool of water arise. It was the swimming pool at his high school gym. He saw students in swimming trunks lining up and he soon recognized himself in the line. His eyes lit up as he realized it was the day of the swim team tryouts. He watched just as the coach appeared. He was a relatively fit White man, in long swimming trunks, a white polo shirt and a red baseball cap. With a clipboard in hand, he walked down the line, asking each student their name and checking it off. When he came to Daniel, he gave Daniel a puzzled look.

"Name?" he asked brusquely.

"Parker," said Daniel confidently as the coach looked puzzled.

"Funny, you don't look like a Parker I've ever seen before."

"My mom's Vietnamese," responded Daniel.

"I see, you're taller than I would expect, must be the other half of ya," said the coach.

Daniel couldn't explain it but the coach's remark stung him, but he didn't let on as he responded, "Yes sir, it must be."

But the memory of what he said and seeing himself saying it jarred Daniel. A deep sense of shame seeped in as he realized he cast aside his Vietnamese half, seeing it as the problem and falling back on his White half. Up until that point in his life, his Vietnamese mother had done everything to support and raise him. In that one moment of insecurity, he had rejected her.

"Are you true?" asked one of the buffalos in Vietnamese.

Daniel grimaced and looked down and uttered, "No. I was not true at that moment."

The water buffalos were unfazed as they all stomped on the ground in unison. The trifecta of hooves caught Daniel's attention as he suddenly focused on the water in the pool. Another ripple started in the center, and another image started to form. His eyes lit up as he saw himself coming back to the Portal Book on that fateful night, after he had failed to manifest the wall Qi element. He felt embarrassed that he didn't know the language of his heritage as well as the other warriors. Yet he was mad too, blaming it on himself for being only half and not having Vietnamese parents who may have had more time to teach him Vietnamese.

But it was surreal for Daniel to see himself in that scene and being able to reflect on the emotions that he was experiencing. Then he remembered feeling determined after the Guardian Buffalo had worked with him earlier. He stood in front of his Portal Book later that night, picking up the Horn Brush and trying again to write the Vietnamese word for wall. Without the distractions of the others around him, he could focus. When he manifested his first Qi element, he felt a sudden surge of happiness as the fiery Vietnamese word flew off the page and seeped into his chest. At that moment, he felt a sudden connection to his heritage. He found purpose for the one factor in his life that caused him to reject and accept himself in a perpetual tug-of-war. Finally, his knowledge of Vietnamese had purpose, him being Vietnamese had purpose, and his identity was no longer a stranger to him.

"Are you true?" asked one of the buffalos in Vietnamese.

Daniel shook his head vigorously and stammered, "Now I am… but I need to be better."

The water buffalos snorted and gazed upward. Daniel was confused and looked up as his jaw dropped. In the ledges above, he saw tens, if not hundreds, of ghostly outlines of water buffalos, all resting on their bellies and looking down at him. *I'm being judged,* he thought, suddenly feeling self-conscious.

"Why are you here?" asked one of the buffalos.

"I came to accompany my friend, the Empress Warrior Wu," said Daniel. "Do you know where she is?"

"Why?" asked another voice.

Daniel was confused by the question. "To protect her and to protect Azen?" he said with an uncertain tone.

"Yes," said a voice from one of the three buffalos but since they could talk only in his mind, none of their mouths moved, so he couldn't tell which one was speaking to him. *"How can you protect her?"*

Daniel thought about the question. He thought about the scenes that the buffalos had shown him. His inner conflicts about his Vietnamese heritage were laid bare for him, and Azen solidified his power of being Vietnamese to protect Azen from the Warlock. But he harkened back to how he wanted to do everything in his power to protect his new buffalo friends and their kingdom. And he realized the answer he needed to give: "By remaining true."

Snorts could be heard from the ledges, and the three buffalos before him simply stared at him.

"Present the Club Horn of KTing Voar over the water," said a voice.

Daniel felt unsure, but he extended the Club Horn of *KTing Voar* over the pool, with the red jade hovering just about its center. The water buffalos to the left and right of him bowed their heads. They slowly moved forward, extending their foreheads until the club horn was gently held in place. The center buffalo moved in and touched his forehead against the red jade. The silence was so thick that Daniel dared not breathe.

Ever so slowly, the three set of horns glowed and pulsated brighter in a rhythmic fashion. Daniel was mesmerized by the scene. His eyes widened as the red jade emitted another white light that seemed to radiate outward, engulfing the room for a split second. The three buffalos slowly pulled back and settled back into their original positions.

Daniel slowly pulled back the club horn and saw no difference. He looked up quickly, expecting one of them to say something about the horn, but instead, he was met with a question in Vietnamese *"What do you call yourself?"*

With reverence, Daniel pulled the club horn across his chest and said solemnly in Vietnamese, "I am Danh Nguyen, proud Vietnamese son of Thuy Nguyen. I am the Emperor Warrior Nguyen of the Buffalo Kingdom of Azen."

There were muffled snorts that caused Daniel to look up as he saw the ghostly bluish silhouettes of the buffalos. They started to vanish until only the three buffalos about the pool remained.

"Remain true," said a voice in his head as the buffalos started to walk backwards into their tunnels.

"I will remain true," said Daniel. "Um wait, how do I find my friend?"

There was no answer as the three buffalos vanished into the tunnels. Only blackness stared back at him. Daniel looked around, then upward into the empty stone ledges and finally back down into the dark, still water in the pool. He lowered the top of the club horn and stared back into the deep red jade and saw that it was back to normal. He slipped the club horn back into the sheath across his back and turned toward the tunnel from which he came from. Before retracing his steps, he paused and whispered *thank you* in Vietnamese, *"cảm ơn bạn."*

He turned around and inhaled the stale air around him as he walked through the tunnel that had so frightened and confused him earlier. With the jade torch in front of him, he simply followed the tunnel and was relieved to find it was neither dissolving nor growing. Being able to see at most ten feet in front of him, his walk was slow and deliberate. After what seemed like an eternity, a faint outline appeared ahead, and his heart raced. He quickened his pace and soon, he passed through the tunnel entrance. He let out a sigh of relief. His ears perked up, causing him to spin around as the tunnel entrance behind him filled with new rock. With a light slap of his palm, he confirmed that it was solid. He quickly looked ahead of him and saw the eerie entrance that Clara had disappeared into. He walked closer to it and saw that a thick, black mist filled in the entire entrance. He tried to push the jade torch into it but could barely get it through. Though it wasn't solid, it was pushing back. He withdrew his hand and exhaled loudly as he let out, "Remain true, Clara!"

THIRTEEN

The darkness slowly closed in on Clara, who sat sorrowfully on the stone floor against the wall with her knees drawn up to her chest. The jade torch she held in front of her was the brightest light in the dark tunnel. Her eyes fell before her and landed nowhere, as there was nothing to see.

Was this the end? she thought. *Was this how the Empress Warrior Wu of the Panda Kingdom was destined to die? Alone in a tunnel with no beginning or end? Where did Daniel go, and what happened to him? Would Yuka and Sung have to fight alone? What would happen to the Panda Kingdom, and what would happen to her Guardian Panda? Did time come to a standstill in this Jade Labyrinth, and she would continue to live out this one singular moment for all of eternity? But her worst fear was, what if she would never be able to see her parents ever again?*

A tear seeped out of the corner of her eye as the sound from her sniffling echoed gently through the tunnel. The tear was followed by a few more streaming down the side of her face, which she wiped away with her hand. One tear escaped down her chin and landed on her jade bracelet snug around the bow, flowing over it. Clara watched the jade bracelet glisten as a pinhead of white light appeared within.

Clara's eyes fixed on the dot of white light, which grew brighter as it emerged out of the jade bracelet itself. It rose as Clara stared at it, her mouth agape. When it had reached eye level, it pulsated for a moment before suddenly flying down the tunnel.

"Wait!" Clara hollered as she bolted upward and started to chase the white bead of light. She approached the jade pebbles that she had dropped onto the ground and ran over them as she followed the white bead. Darkness was all she could see in front of her, and the jade torch showed only more tunnel walls, but she kept after the small white bead of light still zooming ahead of her. She realized that the jade pebbles that she'd placed on the ground didn't reappear, and that perhaps she was no longer running in a circle. *But*, she wondered, *where was the bead of light taking her?*

As she tried to look past the white bead of light, her eyes opened wide as she made out an outline of an exit up ahead. Her pace quickened and she gripped the Bow of Destiny harder as the white bead seemed to stop at the entrance and suddenly shoot straight up and out of sight. Her heart jumped as she raced forward and the outline of the tunnel exit became clear.

Finally, she raced into a square chamber. Her feet came to a halt as the jade torch revealed a circular pool of dark water surrounded by a stone circular wall in the middle of the chamber. Her eyes wandered about the room. Each of the walls had its own tunnel entrance. The chamber was still, as the eerie blackness stared back at her. She raised her jade torch upward to search for the white bead of light when with wonder, she spied tiers of ledges that flared out from the center of the square room. They seemed to go on forever.

"Whoa," Clara said from her breath.

Her ears perked up at a faint, muffled sound, barely audible, coming from one of the tunnels. She extended the jade torch in front of her and saw nothing but utter blackness in the middle entrance.

A sudden noise from the tunnel on the left made her turn as she pointed the jade torch toward it. Then a noise from the right tunnel made her turn in that direction. Her heart raced as she placed her hand onto the grip of her bow.

Her eyes lit up as she saw them: two glowing bluish eyes in the center tunnel. Another set of bluish eyes lit up in the tunnel to her left, and then to her right. She dropped the jade torch as she unslung her bow and loaded an arrow.

With the arrow pointed at the pair of eyes from the center tunnel, she shouted, "Stop!"

Her grip trembled as she drew back on the bow, ready to release it at whatever was about to appear.

Then, it emerged: a large panda, aglow in a bluish light. Her eyes stared on in disbelief and out of the corner of her eyes, similarly large pandas emerged from the tunnels on the left and the right. She relaxed the drawstring as the three pandas looked upon her silently.

"Whoa," she let out as she slid the arrow back into her quiver.

Light seemed to emanate from the tip of each hair of the pandas' shimmering fur, casting an iridescent aura that gently lit the room. Where their fur was white, the tips of the fur glowed brighter, but their eyes were a piercing blue.

They looked at Clara in silence, then bowed in unison toward her.

She suddenly felt self-conscious as she wrestled with the embarrassment of aiming an arrow at a ghostly panda. She put her feet together, straightened up and offered a respectful bow, hoping it would redeem her earlier aggressive gesture. As she straightened up, she was met by their silent gaze.

"Um, I'm Clara," she said as her voice echoed slightly upward. She looked up and suddenly saw dozens of bluish glowing pandas looking solemnly down on her. Her head came back level to the three silent pandas. She suddenly felt out of place until the middle panda brought its paws together.

White wisps started to stream out of the three tunnels and converged around her ankles. Her heart started to race as she shuffled her feet to get away when the middle panda raised his hand, indicating for her to stop. Clara nodded and stood still as she held her bow below her waist. The white wisps started to rise and weave around her legs. As they reached her waist, some branched off and reached over to the jade bracelet. The white wisps finally reached her face, and Clara felt anxious. Suddenly, she was inhaling the white wisps.

She held steady, but she wasn't all too pleased as the white wisps seemed to enter her head and then her mind. For a moment, her vision blurred before clearing up just as the white wisps left her nostrils. They untangled themselves from her body as they retreated into the tunnels from which they came from.

"What do you call yourself?" a voice said in Cantonese.

Clara jumped slightly backward as she quickly turned her head left and right. *Where did that voice come from?* she wondered. Her eyes settled back on the pandas before her as they quietly eyed her.

"Clara, Clara Wu," she said.

The silence was deafening as the voice in her mind said in Cantonese once again, *"What do you call yourself?"*

Clara shook her head slightly and uttered in Cantonese with confidence, "Wu Chu Hua. I am Wu Chu Hua, Empress Warrior Wu of the Panda Kingdom."

"Welcome, Empress Warrior Wu," said the mysterious voice in her head.

"Are you true?"

Her stupefied expression conveyed her blank thoughts as she answered, "I think so?"

There was a silent pause when the paw of the middle panda extended its claws to reveal its open paw. Clara's eyes focused on it as it dipped toward the pool. Clara looked upward awkwardly and moved toward the pool. Something seemed to drop into the center of the pool as she watched the ripples of water expand outward.

Soon an image started to emerge, and she recognized it. It was her family's kitchen. She saw herself at the kitchen table suddenly slamming her knapsack onto the floor. Clara gasped as she suddenly saw herself pick up the old calligraphy book and slam it down onto the kitchen table, causing a bowl of soy sauce to spill all over it. Her mother yelled out, "Clara!" and she was stung to see herself racing out of the kitchen followed by her mother.

She saw herself slamming her bedroom door and throwing herself onto the bed in frustration. Suddenly she saw her mother trying the locked doorknob as she yelled her name again, "Clara!" only to be met with her response that sent shivers down her spine, "I hate being Chinese!"

Watching herself say those words pained her, but it pained her more to see her crestfallen mother hearing those words as she leaned her head against the door. To add more pain to her mother's heart, Clara heard herself say once again, "I hate being Chinese!"

Tears welled up in Clara's eyes and she looked at the three pandas who simply stared at her. The voice asked again in Chinese, *"Are you true?"*

Clara shamefully looked left and right and with an emotional voice uttered, "I didn't mean it! I was mad. I didn't know how I hurt my mother," pleaded Clara.

But the voice in her head came once again, *"Are you true?"*

Clara looked downward and in a shameful voice, "No, not on that day."

The panda on the left opened his paw and directed it downward into the pool. The image of her dejected mother leaning her forehead against her bedroom door sunk into the dark depths as another image started to rise out from the center.

Clara looked down nervously as she watched the image form. She saw herself sitting between the couch and the coffee table. She looked to be about seven years old, and she was busily drawing with markers. Her parents came into the room and quickly settled down on either side of her as they watched their little artist working on her masterpiece. It was a castle, and the main figure seemed to be a princess. Her seven-year-old self suddenly looked up, and her father and mother smiled. She turned her attention to her mother and asked, "Do we have another yellow marker? I can't finish the princess' hair without it."

Her mother smiled and offered, "Why not use a black marker?"

"Princesses don't have black hair, they have blonde hair, it's prettier."

As Clara watched herself burying back into drawing, she saw her mother tug at her own black hair as her father placed his hand on her mother's knee. Her mother looked up at her husband as he whispered, "She'll grow out of it."

But Clara saw her mother's disappointed expression in the water, and Clara's heart sank.

Clara quickly looked up and stammered, "I was seven years old! I didn't mean to say it like that."

Yet the voice in her head came once again, *"Are you true?"*

"Why are you doing this to me? Why are you showing me all the times that I hurt my mother?" Clara pleaded, choking back tears as her lips trembled. Then the troubled thought crept into her mind, *how many other times did she unknowingly hurt her mother?*

The voice persisted in her head and it asked once again, *"Are you true?"*

Clara stomped on the ground in a fit of frustration as her shoulders fell, "No, not on that day. But I didn't know any better! I didn't know what it meant to be Chinese. I don't live in China, I live in New York. Only until I came to Azen did I finally see what it really means to be Chinese. You have to believe me!"

Her passionate voice seemed to fall on deaf furry ears as the pandas stared back at her. The third panda's paw unfurled and directed Clara to the pool once again, and Clara reluctantly looked into it. A third image started to float out of the ripples.

It was her parents, and they were dancing. Clara's frustration was suddenly replaced with amusement as she saw younger versions of her carefree parents. The image of them floated upwards and soon, a pair of Chinese couples appeared beneath her parents. They were young as well, looking into each other's eyes. One man was dressed in a formal army outfit while his female partner was wearing a vintage dress. The other man was wearing a suit while the woman with him wore a Qipao, an elegant Chinese dress. Clara looked at them in puzzlement, and then back at her parents. Her eyes glinted when she realized she was looking at younger versions of her grandparents!

Her eyes darted quickly to the stone-faced bluish pandas, then back to her younger grandparents once more.

"Gong Gong? Po Po?" she muttered in Cantonese as she referred to her maternal grandfather and grandmother. Her eyes shifted to her paternal grandparents as she uttered, "Ye Ye… Ma Ma."

Her eyes gravitated to her maternal grandmother in the Qipao, and she admired how slim and elegant she looked. Her eyes skimmed over to the man in the U.S. army uniform, and she remembered her paternal grandfather was in the U.S. Army. But soon, they were pushed up slowly as four additional pairs of couples appeared beneath her grandparents. Clara was suddenly seeing her great-grandparents in their youth.

Her eyes lit up as she watched them, a line of Chinese men and women, in Mao suits, Chinese styled jackets, farmer attire and one woman in another Qipao styled dress. She knew nothing of her great-grandparents, and seeing them caused her heart to flutter in wonder. But sadness suddenly filled her heart.

"My great-grandparents?" she exclaimed as she looked back at them. "I don't even know how to call you… Where is that Chinese family diagram from Subtle Asian Traits when you need it?"

Her eyes skimmed each person, admiring their facial features, their hairstyles, and soon, she saw them move upward. She looked up and saw the bottom of her parents' soles. With her trembling brown eyes, she desperately reached for the closest pair of great-grandparents and yelled, "Stop!"

A few tense moments passed as Clara fidgeted with her hands, which passed through the closest set of great-grandparents. A slight tingling sensation danced through her hands. The entire line of great-grandparent flickered slightly, and for a fleeting moment, her hands stopped them from rising. She looked down, and she could see yet another line of people starting to take shape beneath them, her great-great-grandparents. She looked desperately at the three pandas and pleaded, "Please, slow it down. I want to see them!"

But she could feel the ephemeral images slipping slowly through her fingers, and her heart raced as tears welled up in her eyes. She didn't know why. As she desperately looked at her great-grandparents, she saw it: On her maternal great-grandmother, she saw a jade bracelet on her left wrist. Her eyes lit up. She scanned the other maternal great-grandmothers, and did not see any bracelets and soon, she could no longer hold them as they ascended, only to be replaced by a whole new line of men and women, all sixteen of them, her great-great-grandparents. She saw farmers, carpenters, artisans, chefs, and the one that caught her attention the most, a woman Kung Fu practitioner.

She shoved her hands into the closest set of great-great-grandparents wanting to prolong the ethereal reunion. Again, Clara scanned the wrists of the Chinese women, and half of the women had jade bracelets, including the woman Kung Fu practitioner. She desperately thought, *which one? Which one was the previous Panda Empress Warrior?*

As her heart pounded, she rejoiced in seeing her great-great-grandparents. But she was also saddened that their stay would be fleeting, and soon they drifted upward as another line of men and women appeared, all thirty-two of her great-great-great grandparents. She saw villagers, stately dressed men, a soldier, a beautiful woman in a style of Chinese dress that she was not familiar with, and so many more. It was all so much to take in as the line of people started to arc around her. As she tried to desperately hold them in place, they drifted upward ever so slowly. She was filled with grief that this would be the first and last time she would see them yet overwhelmed with happy curiosity at the next line of Chinese men and women slowly ascending.

Clara scanned around her as sixty-four great-great-great-great-grandparents rose around her. She timidly wove her hands through the bluish images, desperately trying to slow them down as she admired them. Each time her hand left one person and passed through another, it paused the mysterious upward procession ever so slightly. She knew she couldn't stop it, and the three pandas were not going to slow them down. When she reached the end of the ancestral line on the left, she quickly fanned her hands back the other way to see her other set of great-great-great-great-grandparents along the right.

She smiled at each of them, the ancestors she always honored each year during the Lunar New Year. But this was an empty ceremonial gesture to relatives who lived in a country and time that she had no way to connect to. Still, she did it anyways so that she could enjoy the delicious food that was served aplenty each single Lunar New Year. Each year, the incense burned, fresh oranges appeared as decorations, and the roasted pork with its crackling skin and the tender whole chicken were eaten with smiles, with her extended family of cousins, aunts, uncles, and grandparents.

Clara was distracted from her rush of Lunar New Year memories when she could feel the line of great-great-great-great-grandparents slipping away and upward. She sniffled as she was suddenly looking at one hundred and twenty-eight great-great-great-great-great-grandparents. She took a deep breath and respectfully and curiously looked at each of them, until they floated upward to be replaced by another line of multi-great grandparents. After a while, the last line of her ancestors floated away, their bluish aura dissipating into the darkness above. Her emotions were heavy as Clara rested in a squat, with her hands over her knees as she looked downward, overwhelmed by all that she had seen. The silence was thick, and the bluish glow from the three pandas was steady.

A voice in Clara's mind simply asked, *"Are you true?"*

Clara raked through all the images of generations of grandparents in her mind, hundreds of them. There was no way she could remember them all. Finding the former potential Panda Warrior was not possible as so many of the young Chinese women ancestors had also worn a jade bracelet. The possibility of spotting Hua Mulan eluded her as well. But they left an indelible impression on her as her mind raced backwards, from hundreds, to a hundred, to eight, and then to two, her parents. She realized just then that her very existence was only made possible by the hundreds of Chinese people before her. She nodded gently as she bit her lip and simply said, "I'm Chinese."

The voice spoke once more in her mind, *"Are you true?"*

Clara looked up and gazed into the eyes of the panda on the left, to the right and then the one in the center. She slowly rose and looked at the panda in the center and said *I am Chinese* in Cantonese, *"Ngaw hai joong kwo yan."* And when she heard her say it, she looked at all three glowing pandas and said *I am*

Chinese in Mandarin, "*Wo shi zhong guo ren.*"

The panda on the left opened his other paw and directed Clara to look into the pool. The image that floated upward was recent: It was her in the cafeteria confronting Clarissa. She watched as she hooked Clarissa's leg, causing her to fall. She heard how she confronted Clarissa that Chinese people don't say *ching chong,* to themselves because it meant, "I'm stupid." *A lie, but a good comeback,* she thought. That moment caused onlooking students to laugh at the school bully. Clara couldn't help smiling at the memory when the voice in her head asked, *"Are you true?"*

"That day, I was true," said Clara with a tone of satisfaction. But she suddenly admonished herself and composed her gleeful expression before she looked back up and said calmly, "Yes."

The panda on the right opened his other paw, and Clara looked down at the pool once again. Another image floated upward and she saw herself entering the kitchen with the Portal Book. It was the day she returned from Azen and she had rushed down the hall to apologize to her mother. She saw herself walking nervously into the kitchen and hearing herself say, "I'm sorry." Then more words were exchanged, and she saw herself settling down at the kitchen table as her mother came around. She heard her mother ask, "Where did all this energy come from?" However, hearing her reply made her feel it even more: "Because Mom, I'm proud to be Chinese."

She could anticipate the voice in her head as she looked up, *"Are you true?"*

Clara looked at each of the panda's blank faces and stated, "I am truer today than I was yesterday, and aim to be truer in the days to come. I am Empress Warrior Wu."

The middle panda reached out with both of his open paws and looked at Clara. "*Bow of Destiny,*" he asked in her mind.

Clara nervously fidgeted with the bow in her hands until it was balanced across her two palms. She stepped up to the pool and extended the Bow of Destiny into the bluish palms of the panda. He drew it inward and looked at the hollow that once held the original Bamboo Jade. His thumb grazed the jade bracelet before he looked back up with his bluish eyes.

"I know," Clara said. "Let me explain. I was fighting at our first battle, and a *Huo Dou* Demon Dog bit down on it and it shattered. I saw how all the pandas were defenseless, and in that moment of desperation, I took off that jade bracelet that my mother had given me and slid it onto the bow. I didn't know what I was doing, to be honest, but suddenly it came to life, and it powered up the pandas' battle armor. It was amazing!"

The three pandas looked at Clara until the middle one blinked. *"The Bamboo Jade is no more?"* he asked.

Clara shook her head.

"This jade is not of Azen?" asked the voice in her head.

"No, it was given to me by my mother," said Clara.

The panda looked down at the jade bracelet and placed its paw over it. He closed his eyes and nodded a couple of times. *"It was given by your mother to protect you. By a mother's love to protect her daughter."*

Clara was shaken by the panda's words, and the jade bracelet suddenly had more meaning to her.

The panda extended the Bow of Destiny back to Clara, who took it back into her hands. She looked down at the hollow of the bow and asked, "Can you fix it?"

The three bluish pandas turned their gaze toward each other and closed their eyes. Clara watched silently for about a minute before they reopened their eyes. They rested their gaze on Clara, and she felt the immensity of being judged. She looked up and saw hundreds of blue iridescent pandas looking down at her, making her feel entirely small.

"Remain true," said the voice in her head causing Clara to look back at the three pandas.

Her vision was suddenly disturbed by a flicker from above. She looked up and she saw the bluish pandas vanishing, one by one, until there was none. She cast her eyes back down on the three pandas in front of her only to catch them retreating into their tunnels.

"Wait!" pleaded Clara. "I need you to help me fix the Bow of Destiny!"

But her pleas fell on deaf ears as she raced after the panda on the left who had just entered the tunnel. But as she entered, she saw nothing as the darkness consumed everything. She turned around, and the jade torch on the ground emitted the only light in the dark chamber. She rushed over to it as she yelled into the air, "Wait, please! Was I not true?"

With the jade torch in her hand, she ran toward the tunnel on the right and saw only darkness before her. A sense of hopelessness started to fill the void in her chest as she rushed over to the center tunnel, only to see the same, absolute darkness.

She turned around, feeling rejected as she shook the bow in her left hand. "I failed," said a disappointed Clara. "What am I going to do now?"

She could not stop the sound of her sobbing as she envisioned the impending fate of the pandas. She raised her head as she felt hot tears running down her cheeks. She pondered her failure, in herself, and as a Chinese girl. She nodded in despondent acceptance of her failure and took a step around the pool toward the tunnel from which she came from.

Then, she saw something in the pool, a flicker. She stepped toward the pool and looked directly into the center, and her eyes lit up as something glowed an eerie green. She dropped to her knees and pushed herself up against the stone wall encircling the pool. She slung the bow across her chest and breached the water's surface with her right hand while holding onto the low stone wall with her left. Her fingertips touched the mysterious object, and it flipped over in the pool toward her, glowing an even brighter green. She palmed it and carefully brought it out of the water.

It was a rough piece of green jade.

She smiled with excitement, and all her feelings of hopelessness slipped away. "It's like kryptonite for the Warlock's creatures!" she said with a laugh.

After wiping it down along her training top, she carefully placed it into the pouch that held the other illumination jade pebbles. She pulled the string taut, stood up, and looked into the three dark tunnel entrances. The smile across her face showed heartfelt appreciation as she simply said *thank you* in Cantonese, "*Dò Jeh Sai!*"

Holding the jade torch in front of her, she traversed carefully down the long tunnel that she had entered before she'd gotten separated from Daniel. She was glad that she was not being chased by slithering rock or dissolving solid rock with her bare hands. Something on the ground ahead caught her attention, and she saw the jade pebbles that she had dropped. She knelt, picked them up in her right hand, and admired them before putting them back into the pouch. The light green glow of the new Bamboo Jade gave her reassurance as she continued walking down the tunnel. *It shouldn't be far*, she thought.

It wasn't more than ten feet when her heart skipped a beat upon seeing the outline of the tunnel entrance. She picked up her pace: It was indeed the tunnel entrance. Her anticipation picked up as she finally stepped through and into the tunnel when a voice yelled out, "Clara!"

Daniel suddenly embraced her as she turned to her left. She was taken aback, but she welcomed the hug and chuckled. She patted him on his upper back before he let go and stepped back.

"Are you okay?" he asked urgently.

The profound smile appeared on her tear-stained face as she nodded her head, "Yes, I'm fine."

"What happened in there?" he asked.

Clara paused and turned back to the tunnel entrance that she just stepped through when she saw it sealing up as a new rock face appeared. With a smile, she responded, "Something amazing, but I have something that is even more amazing!"

Daniel watched as she tucked her jade torch under her left armpit. She fiddled with the pouch's drawstring and reached in to withdraw the rough green jade. Daniel's jade torch reflected the deep colors of the green jade and his eyes lit up.

"You found it!" exclaimed Daniel.

Clara nodded happily. "Let's get out of here so that I can get this back to Bamboo Tower."

"You don't have to tell me twice, but before we go, what did you see in there?" asked Daniel.

Clara paused and simply replied, "The truth as to who I am and... how much more I need to become to remain true."

Daniel nodded and added, "Did you have three large bluish water buffalos help you realize that?"

Clara laughed and replied, "No, but I had three large bluish pandas."

Daniel chuckled, "Makes sense. Hey, you didn't by any chance have streams of white fog go up your nose, did you?"

Her laugh was unexpected as she nodded. They began their walk out of the labyrinth, whose tunnels were now free of the slithering rock that had pursued and separated them earlier. They stopped every so often to pick up the jade pebbles that they had dropped along the way. When they came to the last corner of the labyrinth, Daniel reached up and pulled out the arrow, which he gave to Clara, who placed it back in her quiver. They each started to eat a *bao* as they traded stories of their trials when finally, they came across the glowing arrow that Daniel had fashioned with the illumination jade pebbles.

Clara looked back from where they came from and she still had so many questions. *Who were the ephemeral creatures that they had met? Were they ghosts of that reclusive order of Azen monks? Were they some enlightened Azen creatures that found a new form of being? Who built the labyrinth, and how did the tunnels form and reform at will?* As Daniel tossed the last illumination jade pebble into his pouch, he turned to Clara as his jade torch highlighted his features. Clara could better see his almond eyes and the brownish hair that fell across his forehead. She smiled and said, "Let's get out of here."

Daniel smiled and led the way. Soon enough, they could make out the outline of the entrance and they quickened their pace. The pumping of their feet and hearts was amplified in the dark tunnel until finally, they burst through the tunnel and into the illuminated cavern.

"Clara! Daniel!" they heard as they looked around, adjusting their eyes to the light.

Yuka raced toward Clara and threw her arms around her. Sung threw his hands atop Daniel's two shoulders, "Bro, so good to see you!"

The guardians soon fell in from behind as Yuka pulled back from her embrace and uncharacteristically stammered, "What took you so long?"

Clara gave Daniel a confused look before she turned back toward Yuka and said, "What are you talking about? We were only gone for a few hours."

Yuka looked at Sung, who said, "No. You were gone for almost a day!"

Clara and Daniel drew blank faces and looked at each other before the Guardian Panda interrupted, "Empress Warrior Wu, Emperor Warrior Nguyen, welcome back. We are glad you are safe, no matter how much time may have passed. How was your task?"

Clara smiled as she loosened the drawstring, reached in with her right hand, and proudly withdrew the rough green jade stone.

Everyone's jaws dropped as they stared at the glimmering green jade stone. "Yeah! You found it!" Yuka happily yelled out.

"Excellent work, Empress Warrior Wu. I had no doubt," lauded the Guardian Panda. "We must hurry back, there is no time to waste. Hurry, please."

The urgency in the Guardian Panda's voice could be felt. Everyone waited for the stone slab to be pushed back into place and the four keys returned to each guardian. They made their way out of the mine, and once outside of the mine's entrance, they harnessed themselves onto their feathered aviators and flew off for Bamboo City.

FOURTEEN

"How much longer?" asked Sung as he paced in place in Clara's room at Bamboo Tower.

Clara looked up from her sitting position from her bed and said, "I don't know."

"It's been like three hours now since we've returned, and when you handed over the green jade to that panda with the white beard," said Sung.

"I love how peaceful it is here," Yuka interrupted, who was leaning by the window with Daniel.

"It's pretty amazing," said Clara with a smile. "I'm glad you could all come by and check out Bamboo City."

"We should all try to visit each other's kingdoms!" exclaimed Sung. "The view from the top of Claw Mountain is pretty amazing."

"But isn't it cold there?" asked Daniel.

"It is, but only near the top of the mountain," Sung answered. "Besides, there are tons of fireplaces. You can literally walk into mine."

"Don't you think it's odd that the water Wu warrior is surrounded by fire and me being the fire Wu warrior, I'm surrounded by water?" asked Daniel.

Clara and Yuka looked at Sung as he paused, "You're right! I never thought of that!"

"Fire..." said Daniel as he turned and pointed at Sung who responded resoundingly, "and Ice!"

As the guys laughed, Yuka gave Clara an annoyed look before they both laughed.

"So, you can't tell us what you saw in the Jade Labyrinth?" asked Yuka as she walked towards the bed.

Clara looked up at Yuka's inquisitive eyes as she settled onto the bed in front of her. She glanced over at Daniel who stared silently back and turned back to Yuka. "No, I don't think I should," said Clara disappointedly. "But I so want to!"

Daniel laughed and uttered, "Oh my god, I so want to as well, but I can't."

"Come on, we're your fellow warriors! We can keep a secret," said Sung teasingly.

"It's not that," said Clara. "We simply can't, for the good of Azen."

There was a moment of silence before Sung said, "Wow, that's pretty heavy."

"Was it scary?" asked Yuka?

"Oh, it was! Right, Daniel?" said Clara as she turned to Daniel.

"Damn right it was!" Daniel exclaimed.

"But once I realized I didn't need to be scared anymore, I just had to remain true," said Clara.

"What does that mean?" asked Yuka.

Clara smiled, "Like Emperor Warrior Hong said to the rest of the warriors who followed into the Jade Labyrinth after him, just 'remain true.'" Her voice trailed off in a low tone.

Yuka listened to every word in wonder and was broken out of her trance when Sung said, "So dramatic. Like a K-Drama!"

The collective laugh was shared, and Sung continued, "So Clara got a new jade stone, and please God, let it work. But what did you get?"

Daniel looked at Sung and paused. He unsheathed the club horn from his back and placed the tapered end on the ground in front of him as he held the top of the horn that contained the red jade. It glistened back at him as he looked back at Sung, "I didn't get anything, but maybe, I got some perspective?"

"Oh, you two are impossible!" said Sung as he brought his hands up in animated frustration. "And now you sound like a fortune cookie!"

More laughter ensued when a knock at the door caught their attention. As the door slid opened, the warriors collected themselves as both Clara and Yuka hopped off the bed. The Guardian Panda entered the room and offered a slight bow that the others reciprocated.

"Empress and emperor warriors," said the Guardian Panda with a hint of reservation. "We are ready, Empress Warrior Wu, please follow."

Clara nodded, slipped into her boots, and quickly followed the Guardian Panda as the rest of the warriors trailed after her.

With the Guardian Panda and Clara on one side, the three warriors squeezed into the other side of the lift as it descended. The collective nervous silence was evident as Clara started to feel the uncertainly in her mind. The lift stopped as she looked out and saw that they had reached the Jade Floor. The Guardian Panda stepped off, followed by the rest of the warriors.

Yuka's, Sung's, and Daniel's eyes stared in wondrous amazement as they took in the light green glow and surveyed the hundreds of pandas busily grinding away at jade pieces. A couple of panda attendants greeted them and handed everyone a mask, which they put on. The Guardian Panda motioned for everyone to follow.

"Wow," muttered Sung through his mask as his eyes took in everything on the floor. "This is so cool."

"You have something similar at Claw Mountain." said the Guardian Panda. "You all do."

"I need to get my Guardian Tiger to show me," said Sung.

They soon came upon a circular glass room whose glass door slid open. Everyone stepped through as an attendant slid it closed. Before them by the large circular bamboo table were the Head of the Pandemonium Squad, the Jadeologist, and the Panderess. As the Guardian Panda bowed, the warriors followed suit and the Panderess nodded slightly. She motioned her paw to her face, and they all took off their face masks, which were collected by a panda attendant.

"Empress Warrior Wu and fellow empress and emperor warriors," said the Panderess in a stately manner. "Thank you for your patience…"

"Oh, this is so exciting to have all the warriors here in my lab!" the Jadeologist interrupted excitedly.

"Le Le," chided the Panderess.

"Oh, my apologies, my Panderess," said the Jadeologist apologetically.

"It's okay. It's understandable that you are excited," said the Panderess with a smile as she continued. "First, I am so relieved that our Empress Warrior Wu has returned safely from the Forbidden Cave of Jade Mountain, and I want to thank you, Emperor Warrior Nguyen for accompanying our Panda Warrior on her mission. The bravery of both of you is enormously appreciated."

"Thank you," said Clara followed by Daniel, who said, "Yes, thank you."

"Jadeologist, I'll turn it over to you," said the Panderess.

"Thank you, Panderess," said the Jadeologist respectfully. "I have to admit, I was so excited to have the new jade stone in my hand. I even got to use the original cast that was used for the previous Bamboo Jade to shape the new jade stone to fit into the Bow of Destiny. I had to retrieve it from the archives. That was so exciting! Never did I think it would be used again! We would be in a tough bamboo if the new Bamboo Jade didn't fit, and since we only had the one to work with, I would not be able to reshape another one. We would have been quite bamboozled and that may have forced you into another mission…"

"Jadeologist," admonished the Panderess. "Focus."

"Oh yes," said the Jadeologist. "Well, needless to say, I was able to finely craft a new Bamboo Jade."

The Jadeologist stepped aside and behind him on the table was a gleaming green jade stone. It was held up by a pair of calipers and it was gleamingly beautifully.

Clara's eyes fell upon it as she let out, "Wow."

"Yes, beautiful, isn't it?" said the Jadeologist proudly. "It is my finest work."

"Does it work?" asked Clara.

The Jadeologist looked up at the Panderess and looked at the Bow of Destiny that was resting on a rack a few feet away along the table. He waddled over to it and gingerly lifted it off and walked back toward the group. The Jadeologist carefully unhooked the drawstring at each end of the bow. He carefully placed his paw over the jade bracelet and gently twisted it off. His furry paw carefully placed it on a red bamboo silk cloth. The glowing jade that hung around the Guardian Panda, the one embedded in the armor of the Head of the Pandemonium Squad and the one around the Panderess' neck, all faded. Soon, all the green jade in the lab lost its glow, and all the outside noise from the jade grinding suddenly stopped.

The Head of the Pandemonium Squad looked down at his idle jade as his eyes blinked a few times, knowing that the protection of the jade was gone, once again.

"Three things must come together to invoke the power of the Bamboo Jade," said the Jadeologist. "The Bamboo Jade, the Bow of Destiny, and the Qi of the Panda Warrior."

The Jadeologist carefully rested the unadorned bow onto a rack, inspected the hollow and blew on it. With a pair of chopsticks, he plucked the new Bamboo Jade from the calipers and carefully inserted it into the hollow. With a press of his thumb, it snapped in snugly with an audible click. The Jadeologist exhaled a sigh of relief and polished it quickly with a cloth. He admired the shiny Bamboo Jade in the Bow of Destiny and reattached the drawstring. Holding the bow with both hands, he turned carefully and presented it to Clara.

Clara stepped forward and gingerly accepted the Bow of Destiny. She exhaled and looked down at the new Bamboo Jade. Like its predecessor, it was beautiful. With the slight twist of the bow, the new jade caught the light from the illumination jade above, but no magical white light spiraled out of it.

Clara looked up, bewildered, and everyone else looked up at each other. The Panderess looked down at her dull jade around her neck.

"Perhaps you need to touch it?" asked the Jadeologist.

Clara nodded and placed her hand over the lower part of the Bamboo Jade as she regripped the bow. But still, nothing.

Clara's mind started to race as she wondered what was wrong. She didn't recall any instructions offered by the three ghostly pandas. Panic started to creep in as she feared for the pandas' survival without the protective power of the Bamboo Jade. Her mind revisited her time in the Jade Labyrinth as thoughts rested on the only resounding phrase "Remain true."

Clara looked up and saw the concerned looks on everyone's faces. But she composed herself and took a step back. She looked at everyone and stared back into the eyes of the Guardian Panda.

With the bow in hand, she thrust it upward and exclaimed in Mandarin, *"I am Wu Chu Hua, Empress Warrior Wu of the Panda Kingdom."*

With the new Bamboo Jade thrust high, a white light suddenly erupted from it and in an instant, it radiated outward, illuminating all the green jade in the Panda Kingdom.

Clara brought the Bow of Destiny back down and could see that the Bamboo Jade was aglow, and she smiled with relief. She looked up and saw that the jades adorning the Panderess, the Guardian Panda and the Head of the Pandemonium Squad were again aglow.

Sung and Daniel fist bumped each other as Yuka clapped quietly in place.

"Well done," said the Panderess as she nodded appreciatively.

"Well done indeed," exclaimed the Jadeologist. "I was about to wet my fur!"

Everyone let out a laugh as the Guardian Panda looked at the Head of the Pandemonium Squad, who whispered snidely into the Guardian Panda's ear as he headed out, "I don't want to admit it, but he said it for all of us."

The Jadeologist picked up Clara's jade bracelet and turned to her. "I'll take your Azen jade bracelet now."

Clara nodded as she slung the Bow of Destiny around her chest. It took her a minute of pulling with pursed lips to wrestle the Azen jade bracelet from her wrist. She handed it to the Jadeologist, who extended to her the jade bracelet her mother had given her.

"Treasure that," said the Jadeologist as she watched Clara slide it back onto her wrist. "That is a special earthen jade with Azen powers."

Clara looked at the jade bracelet more fondly and looked back up at the

Jadeologist, "I will. It is special."

"Well, now that the power of the green jade is restored, empress and emperor warriors, please get ready for your trip to your kingdoms and..." said the Panderess before she paused as she eyed Clara's raised hand. "Yes, Empress Warrior Wu?"

"I don't mean to interrupt, Panderess," said Clara. "But would you mind if I have the Azen jade bracelet?"

The Jadeologist looked down at the Azen bracelet that he had fashioned and looked back up toward the Panderess, who said, "I don't see why not."

The Jadeologist smiled and stepped forward to a grinning Clara who reached out for it with both her hands. She looked down at it and looked back up as she said, "*Dò Jeh!*"

"Oh! You speak Cantonese too? Well, you are most welcome, Empress Warrior Wu," said the Jadeologist. "It is an honor that you would have one of my creations, please cherish it."

"I will," said Clara.

"Well then," said the Panderess. "Cranes will bring you back to your respective kingdoms for the night and you'll recommence with your training tomorrow. The next battle is upon us."

FIFTEEN

"Whoosh!" shouted Clara as she pretended to release an arrow from the Bow of Destiny as the new Bamboo Jade glowed. She spun around, rolled onto and off the bed, landed on one knee with her other leg propped up as she imagined releasing yet another arrow. "Whoosh!" she let out with a smile.

Her eyes lit up as a knock came on the door. She quickly straightened up as it slid open.

"Hey," said Daniel hesitantly.

Clara had just brought the Bow of Destiny down in front of her when she answered, "Oh hey! I was just admiring the new Bamboo Jade." She brushed her hair backwards and over her shoulder as Daniel slipped out of his boots.

"Yuka and Sung already flew back to their kingdoms. Um, I can't stay long since Guardian Buffalo is waiting for me, but I wanted to see you before I left."

Clara gestured to the corner of her bed as she laid the bow down on it while sitting diagonally from Daniel.

"What a trip," said Daniel. "Jade Labyrinth…"

"Yah," echoed Clara. "It was for me as well."

"So, one thing that I didn't mention," said Daniel before he paused. "They knew that I was half Vietnamese."

Clara paused as she caught Daniel looking away. "They did?"

Daniel let out a sigh and uttered, "Yah, they did. But they showed me parts of my life that I didn't know about. I didn't know that my mom had to put up with so much from jerks but protected me at the same time. That really hurt."

"Oh, I'm so sorry, Daniel," said Clara.

"Yah, I didn't know that I was putting down my Vietnamese side when I was trying to fit in. I just never knew how to be proud of it, but when I'm with my mom, it's all I know," said Daniel. "But all my life, I just felt it wasn't the best part of me even though I love my mom, who's always stayed with me."

"Hey, I know how you feel. I have doubts too," offered Clara.

"But you're full Chinese," said Daniel. "How do you know?"

Clara pursed her lips and began, "That's what makes it worse. I am 100% Chinese, but I haven't always been proud of being Chinese. It feels like a burden sometimes, you know. But then the pandas, they showed me... how I hurt my parents. And I didn't mean to. But you know, we live in America, and nothing tells us that we're cool. You know?"

"Huh... I never thought of it that way. Being half, I always envied those Asians who were full Asians. You had Asian parents, you hung out with each other. Being half, it was tough to belong, and I guess I did the worst thing. I tried to belong to another group by making fun of my Vietnamese side. Man, that's so screwed up!"

"Hey, at least you have half to reject!" Clara joined in jokingly. "I would have to reject 100% of myself!"

They chuckled at her epiphany.

"But being here on Azen," continued Daniel. "It's all that matters, and I know it matters."

"Same!" said Clara. "I finally feel that I can be that Chinese girl that I kind of always left behind in the shadows."

"Chinese empress," said Daniel teasingly.

Clara jovially pointed her finger at Daniel, "Yes, Chinese empress! Mr. Vietnamese emperor!"

Daniel chuckled as he bowed slightly to Clara, who mimicked the gesture.

"Did I tell you? I made my dad call me 'Empress' instead of 'Princess!'" said Clara.

"Really? A little flex there!" Daniel said teasingly.

"Yah, because I realized princesses are for White girls, empresses are for Asian girls," Clara said proudly.

"Maybe I should make my mom call me 'Emperor,'" said Daniel.

"No," interjected Clara curtly. "It doesn't work the same for boys."

Daniel chuckled and nodded in agreement as he continued, "Yah, but still, I wouldn't give up the title of Emperor Warrior Nguyen. That's just dope!"

"I love my title, Empress Warrior Wu!" Clara said gleefully as she swayed slightly from side-to-side.

"Hey, before I go," said Daniel. "I didn't mean to make you choose between me and Sung. I just went back to doubting my Vietnamese half, and thought you doubted it too."

"It's okay," said Clara soothingly. "I'm glad I changed my mind."

"I'm glad, too," said Daniel. "Those water buffalos really showed me a side that I never got to see. Being half Vietnamese, uh, I did it again. Being Vietnamese is amazing," said Daniel with newfound pride.

"And you should be," said Clara. "Because you are Emperor Warrior Nguyen of the Buffalo Kingdom!"

Daniel bowed his head as she smirked. "That I am. Thanks for chatting, I'll see you tomorrow morning."

Clara looked up at Daniel as he got up and replied, "Yep, you will. To save Azen!"

As Daniel walked toward the door, he looked back at Clara and remarked, "You should check out my room at the Buffalo Kingdom. It's water everywhere!"

Clara smiled, "I'd love to!"

"Night," said Daniel as he slipped into his boots and left Clara's room. She nodded and turned toward the evening view from Bamboo Tower.

SIXTEEN

The warriors stood by their Portal Books the next morning busily manifesting Qi elements. The next battle was looming, and they couldn't afford to be without their Qi elemental powers. They looked up when they heard the trudging feet of their guardians.

Clara straightened up, placed her bamboo brush at the top of the Portal Book, and pulled taut her training top along its magnetic edging. The Guardian Buffalo, Tiger, and Crane walked over to their warriors and offered greetings. The Guardian Panda nodded his head at Clara as he stepped into the middle of the circle.

"Good morning, empress and emperor warriors," said the Guardian Panda as the warriors responded in unison. "Though you were called back early to assist with the search for the new Bamboo Jade for the Bow of Destiny, I hope that you have been spending time back on your earthly world manifesting your Qi elements. Good. To continue your training, your guardians and I will teach you new Qi elements that we have seen from other previous warriors. It is our experience that not every empress or emperor warrior can manifest all the Qi elemental powers of their Wu element. It has nothing to do with penmanship, and we cannot explain why. That is between you and the Portal Book."

Sung raised his hand and the Guardian Panda nodded at him. "So, we may not be able to invoke all the Qi elements of previous warriors?"

"Yes," responded the Guardian Panda. "Previous warriors were also not able to manifest all the collective Qi elements that we have observed or cataloged over the past hundreds of years. Yes?" said the Guardian Panda as he deferred to Clara's raised hand.

"How old are you, Guardian Panda?" she asked innocently.

The Guardian Panda's brown eyes blinked a couple of times as he looked around to his fellow guardians, who wore collective expressions from aloofness to amusement.

"She asked you first," said the Guardian Tiger in a snarky tone.

"A lot older than you…" said the Guardian Panda to Clara before the

Guardian Tiger, interjected with a hearty laugh, "He's the oldest one here, our esteemed Guardian Panda."

"You are not that far behind, old friend," said the Guardian Panda over the light chorus of laughter from the other guardians. "As I was saying, Empress Warrior Wu, I'm old enough to have seen enough, and the Qi elements that we have taught you so far have been successfully manifested by all warriors in the past. Over the next few days, we're going to see which other Qi elements you are able to manifest."

"So, warriors," the Guardian Tiger bellowed out. "Emperor Warrior Kim, please recite for me the Qi elements that you have manifested so far in the order that you manifested them."

Sung shook his head and began, "Wall..." But the Guardian Tiger stopped him and said, "In Korean."

Sung nodded in acknowledgement, "Oh yes." He took in a breath and in Korean, recited *wall, evaporate, icicle,* and *bridge*: "*dahm, salajida, godeuleum, dali.*"

The Guardian Tiger nodded and looked over at the Guardian Crane, who asked, "Empress Warrior Satoh, the same please."

Yuka confidently composed herself and recited in Japanese *wall, vacuum, gust,* and *fly*: "*kabe, kuukan, toppū, tobu.*"

The Guardian Crane nodded and looked over at the Guardian Buffalo who asked, "Emperor Warrior Nguyen, the same please."

Daniel inhaled and in his best Vietnamese recited *wall, extinguish, fireball,* and *thrust*: "*tường, dập tắt, quả cầu lửa, đẩy.*"

"Very good, Emperor Warrior Nguyen. Your Vietnamese has gotten much better," the Guardian Buffalo said.

Daniel's smile could have lit up a room as he said *thank you* in Vietnamese, "*cảm ơn bạn.*"

"And now that leaves you, Empress Warrior Wu," said the Guardian Panda.

Clara cleared her throat and recited confidently in Cantonese *wall, flatten, split,* and *sinkhole*: "*teng-bin, gum-bin, fun-hoi, tei-hum.*"

The Guardian Panda paused as he looked at Clara. Expecting an acknowledgement, Clara turned her head toward him with an expression of uncertainty. He continued, "Good. Now in Mandarin as well."

Clara realized her double duty but faced forward and confidently recited in Mandarin the same words, "*qiǎng, yā píng, fēnliè, tiān kēng.*"

"Whoa, two languages? Now I'm really glad I'm Vietnamese," Daniel mouthed under his breath in disbelief.

"Very good, Empress Warrior Wu," said the Guardian Panda. "Now, we'll work with you to enhance your Qi elemental powers."

The warriors nodded as they turned to their guardians. Clara's eyes followed the Guardian Panda until he stood in front of the Portal Book stone tablet. He looked at her with his brown eyes and simply said, "Mud."

Clara looked vexed as she repeated back to him, "Mud?"

"Yes. Mud. It's a great Qi element that lets you turn the terrain under your enemy to mud. It slows them down immediately," said the Guardian Panda.

Clara nodded as she picked up her brush, turned to a new page, and began to brush the character for "mud."

"I got it! I got tornado!" exclaimed Yuka as the reddish-orange Japanese character for tornado floated toward her chest and seeped in.

As if on cue, Sung yelled out, "Awesome! I just manifested wave!"

Daniel smiled as he went back to work on, "stream."

Feeling under pressure, Clara went back to manifesting the character for mud. But after the twentieth attempt, none of the black characters turned into fiery embers. Her consternation showed on her face, and she was befuddled as to why she couldn't manifest it. She sighed.

"Try pillar," said the Guardian Panda.

"Huh?" asked Clara. "Pillar? What would a pillar of dirt do in battle?"

"You can send yourself up on a pillar of dirt out of harm's way or send your enemy up on a pillar of dirt, trapping them," the Guardian Panda answered.

Clara nodded in understanding. She exhaled, still perturbed that she could not manifest such a simple Chinese character as mud. With her brush, she delicately brushed out the strokes for pillar, and it manifested immediately. As the fiery embers within the black strokes came to life, she smiled as the reddish-orange character lifted off the page and seeped into her chest.

"That was easy," said Clara.

"Excellent, Empress Warrior Wu. Now continue to manifest more and add it to your arsenal of Qi elemental powers," advised the Guardian Panda.

Clara focused on brushing out the character for pillar when she heard from Daniel, "Finally! I got stream! Yes!"

Clara chimed in, "I got pillar!" In her mind, she knew that her fellow warriors were wondering what kind of pillar it was, but she didn't want them to think that she hadn't manifested anything. She continued to manifest as the morning wore on.

* * *

"Oh my god, this baguette is so warm and fluffy. Awesome *banh mi* again!" raved Daniel as his eyes closed to enjoy the taste of the tofu *banh mi* sandwich that was served during lunch.

"It is pretty good," said Yuka as she finished swallowing a bite, her tastebuds were tickled by the pickled vegetables.

"Well, not as good as what my *mẹ* and I make," said Daniel. "When I was kid, she would buy ingredients after work on a Friday. Then she would make fresh baguette on Saturday, and we build *banh mi* sandwiches together. Those were fun times."

"Do you still make them with your mom?" asked Sung.

As Daniel chewed and swallowed another bite, he nodded for a moment as he placed one finger up and began, "Well, not as much as before. Being on the swim team, one *bahn mi* wouldn't be enough."

"So, eat two," said Sung snidely as the entire table chuckled.

"But yah, you know, you're right. I'm going to make *banh mi* with my *mẹ* again," said Daniel. "I really enjoyed those times."

"Oh, that is so sweet!" exclaimed Clara. "Isn't that so, Yuka?"

Yuka had just chewed off another bite of her *banh mi* as she turned to Clara nodding in agreement.

"You know, when I get back home, I'm going to make some dumplings with my parents," said Clara. "I used to make them with my parents when I was a kid."

"My dad would let me grill the *kalbi* with him over the barbecue, but I never learned how to make *gimbap*. My mom makes all of those," said Sung.

"What's a *gimbap*?" asked Yuka.

"Oh, it's like a *makimono* roll," Sung responded. "It's rolled up in seaweed too, but everything inside is cooked."

"Oh," said Yuka as she envisioned the *gimbap* in her mind.

"Warriors," said the Guardian Panda. "It's wonderful to hear of your cooking stories with your parents. However, you need to finish up soon so that we may continue with your training today. This afternoon's training will be warrior pairing."

All the warrior's eyes lit up as they looked at each other and wondered what the Guardian Panda meant by warrior pairing.

* * *

The warriors were gathered at the Gauntlet along with their guardians. The Guardian Panda stepped out and addressed the warriors.

"Empress and emperor warriors," he said firmly. "Warrior pair training is your ability to work with another warrior and combine your Qi elemental powers. No one Wu pair is better than any other, but this is another skill to have when a situation may present itself on the battlefield. This was already exhibited by the fire and air Wu working together in the first battle, when Empress Warrior Satoh and Emperor Warrior Nguyen worked together to erect air and fire walls to confuse the *Huo Dou* Fire Demon dogs. Now we want to hone that warrior pairing."

The Guardian Tiger stepped forward. "Let's have Empress Warrior Wu and Emperor Warrior Kim step forward."

Both Clara and Sung eagerly stepped up and stood next to each other. They looked at each other, smiled, and focused on the Guardian Tiger.

"Empress Warrior Wu," said Guardian Tiger. "As you just learned to manifest the Qi element for pillar, please invoke a pillar to rise up on."

Clara nodded, walked out and faced everyone. She exhaled and she conjured the Qi elemental power for *pillar*, "*chu.*" The bluish character danced on her fingertips. She admired the new Qi element and clenched her first downward as the bluish character shot down into the earth. Immediately, the earth beneath Clara rose in a pillar about six feet in diameter. As the pillar rose, Clara was caught off guard and abruptly fell onto all fours to balance herself as the pillar rumbled upwards. She closed her eyes as her heart raced until finally the rumbling stopped. She slowly opened her eyes as her breathing picked up.

"Empress Warrior Wu!" said one of the guardians from below. "Are you all right?"

Clara slowly looked around and saw that she had a commanding view of the terrain. She slowly worked herself to the edge of the pillar, looked down, and gulped. She was some fifty feet up and saw her fellow warriors and guardians below.

"Empress Warrior Wu, are you all right?" asked the Guardian Tiger.

"Yes! Yes I am," said Clara. "I'm just afraid of heights."

Sung immediately swung into action and invoked the bridge Qi element, spiraling upward and around the earthen pillar until he reached Clara. He carefully stepped off as Clara looked up at him. He knelt and said soothingly, "Hey, it's okay."

Clara smiled, "I feel so silly. I didn't know I was going to rise up so fast and high."

"That was pretty cool, though!" said Sung. "But you want to know how you can get back down?"

"I'm not sure if I want to flatten the pillar when I'm on it," said Clara cautiously.

"Or you can use the cool ice slide," said Sung teasingly as he motioned with his eyes toward the ice bridge that spiraled downward around the dirt pillar. Clara's eyes lit up.

As everyone on the ground looked up, they suddenly heard laughter coming from above and soon, the warriors and guardians caught sight of Clara sliding down the spiral ice slide with her hands up. Close behind was an enthusiastic Sung. As she reached the end, Clara hopped off and landed on her two feet with a laugh. Sung also hopped away and ended up close to Clara, who was still laughing.

"Warriors…" said the Guardian Tiger.

But before he could finish, Daniel interjected, "No way! Yuka, let's go!"

Daniel and Yuka invoked their Qi elemental powers and soared upward before their guardians could protest. Soon, a giggling Yuka was sliding down the spiral ice slide followed by Daniel, laughing in tandem. They soon landed and hopped away as Yuka exclaimed as she giggled, "I'm all wet!"

"Ahem," said the Guardian Tiger with the other guardians close behind him.

The warriors suddenly recomposed themselves as they realized their quick childish diversion took time away from the training. The Guardian Tiger raised one of his eyebrows and said, "Emperor and empress warriors, that was good collaboration, but maybe not one suited for battle."

The warriors shifted slightly and grinned at being chastised by the Guardian Tiger.

"Emperor Warrior Kim and Empress Warrior Wu," said the Guardian Tiger. "Split the earth and fill it with upright icicles."

Clara and Sung nodded and walked ahead of the others. Standing side-by-side and giving each other a glance, Clara split the earth about fifty feet in length and ten feet wide. She looked at Sung, who quickly invoked around fifty icicles that sprung upright from the depth of the split earth.

"Man, that's a lot of work for me," said an exhausted Sung. "Imagine if we could use both hands to invoke our powers. But you know what, it's not done. It's too obvious that it's a trap."

Sung invoked the bridge Qi element and spanned the split with a thin sheet of ice that would break away under the weight of unsuspecting enemies.

"It's still too obvious," said Clara as she invoked the Qi elemental power for wall and a low dirt wall rose over the ice sheet. Then, with the flatten Qi element, she flattened the dirt wall to obscure the ice sheet beneath it.

"Excellent!" exclaimed the Guardian Tiger. "Emperor Warrior Kim and Empress Warrior Wu, you didn't even need any coaching from myself or the Guardian Panda. You two instinctively knew how to forge your warrior pairing to create something suitable for the battlefield."

"Very good," said the Guardian Panda.

"Thank you," said Clara and Sung, feeling both embarrassed by and appreciative of the praise.

"Empress Warrior Satoh and Emperor Warrior Nguyen, your guardians will take you to the far end of the Gauntlet and work on your warrior pairing. We'll switch off and create new pairs later," the Guardian Tiger instructed.

Both Yuka and Daniel nodded and headed down the Gauntlet with their guardians as the Guardian Tiger and Panda focused on Sung and Clara.

"We'll name off a pair of Qi elements, and you two will use your imagination to pair them up," said the Guardian Tiger.

Both Clara and Sung nodded and stepped ahead of the guardians. From behind, they heard, "Pillar and bridge."

Clara looked at Sung and created a single dirt pillar while looking confounded.

"He wants me to create an ice bridge," said Sung. "So maybe create another pillar?"

Clara nodded and created a twin pillar about twenty-five feet away from the first. Sung spanned an ice bridge between the two pillars that glistened in the sun. Both Clara and Sung admired their work. Then Sung asked, "But how do we use this in battle?"

They pondered for a few seconds when Clara excitedly said, "I know!"

Without hesitation, she quickly invoked the flatten Qi elemental power, and the two dirt pillars collapsed to the ground, causing the ice bridge to crumble violently onto the earth.

"Awesome!" said Sung. "Another trap!"

The Guardian Tiger and Panda looked on approvingly as the Guardian Panda said, "They figured it out."

Suddenly, the wind whipped around them, and squinting, they could see up ahead a tight tornado. It spun around in place under Yuka's control, and suddenly, it was ablaze as Daniel infused it with a stream of fire. They had created a fiery tornado!

SEVENTEEN

Later that night, Sung found himself restless. He paced around his tent quarters and even though he had eaten dinner, he was craving a snack. He stepped over to the tent entrance and slipped into his boots, imagining what late-night snacks he may be able to snag. He exited his tent as the Claw Staff laid on his bed. A nearby white tiger guard was roaming about and reared its head as it stared at Sung with its piercing eyes.

"*Annyeonghaseyo,* I'm just going down to the meal prep area to see if they have anything to eat," said Sung reassuringly.

The tiger nodded and responded, "Very well, Emperor Warrior Kim." He continued his patrol route as Sung walked away.

It was a calm and warm night, which soothed Sung's restlessness. He wondered what the other warriors were up to. As he approached the meal prep area, a white tiger attendant saw him approach and briskly approached him.

The tiger attendant, was smaller in stature than the Guardian Tiger, bowed slightly as Sung responded in kind.

"*Annyeonghaseyo,*" the tiger greeted. "How may I help you, Emperor Warrior Kim?"

Sung smiled as he could never find it boring to have a tiger speak to him in Korean. "*Annyeonghaseyo!* I was wondering if there was anything to snack on?"

The tiger attendant smiled and responded, "It's no trouble. We have leftovers from tonight's dinner, unless you would like me to make you something special?"

"Oh please, no," said Sung. "Leftovers are fine."

The tiger nodded and directed Sung to follow her. She came to a table where there were several bamboo boxes. She pulled one out and flipped it open, "Dumplings?"

Sung shook his head politely. The tiger attendant closed the lid and pulled another bamboo box to reveal a few bamboo *baos*, to which Sung also declined. On the third box, as she opened it, a familiar smell entered Sung's nostrils as she presented a box filled with slices of *kimchi* pancake. Sung's eyes lit up and nodded eagerly.

The tiger's eyes blinked and asked, "Would you like all of it?"

"Oh no, four slices maybe?"

"Certainly," said the tiger as she eased out four of the crispiest slices with a pair of chopsticks onto a bamboo sheet. She quickly folded it and reached over for a bamboo thermos, uncapped it, and filled it with water from a bamboo jug. With the bamboo thermos capped, she presented both to Sung.

"*Gam-sa-ham-ni-da*," Sung thanked her and expressed appreciatively with a slight bow.

The tiger also bowed and responded, "It was my pleasure, Emperor Warrior Kim. Eat well."

Sung turned happily away and eagerly opened the bamboo paper packaging. Under the moonlight, he could see the four triangular pieces of *kimchi* pancake. He could smell the fresh *kimchi* along with the lingering scent of the oil used to fry it. He tore off the top of one and shoved it into this mouth, and the flavor immediately shook him out of his listlessness. He felt a sudden bounce in his step as he walked along the path.

The White Tiger tent compound was in front of him. He had devoured two more slices before he stopped. He exhaled and looked up into the night sky. He was still amazed by the large gaseous-purplish planet that was in plain view, even though it was millions of miles away. His eyes bounced from one moon to another. He wondered which one would be next for the lunar eclipse.

He gazed toward the tent quarters when his eyes wandered over to another nearby path. He was pensive for a moment before he quickly ducked off the main path and took the other. His pace quickened as he surreptitiously made his way to the Origins Pool.

As he cleared the bamboo path, the serene Origins Pool came into sight. The water was still, and it reflected the celestial night sky. Sung looked to each side and saw no one else. He crossed the ground and came to the edge of the pool. He knelt by the stone wall and placed the remainder of the *kimchi* pancake and the bamboo thermos on the pool's stone rim. He looked deep into the still water and exhaled as his expression turned to one of annoyance.

His tense hands went to his temples as he let out a frustrated grunt. Soon his palms came to rest on the stone wall as he looked out into the dark still water. "I totally forgot to bring my staff," he said underneath his breath in disbelief. "I'll guess I'll conjure you up tomorrow, *appa*."

A twig suddenly snapped, and leaves rustled as Sung's eyes darted toward a ghostly figure in the bamboo stalks to his right. He straightened up and peered into the darkness of the stalks when something in white sprinted behind another large bamboo stalk. Sung raced toward it, and suddenly, the ghostly figure darted deeper into the bamboo forest.

"Hey!" hollered Sung as he gave chase. "Stop!"

Whoever it was, it was effortlessly weaving through the bamboo stalks up ahead. But its white robe made it stand out. Sung conjured up the bridge Qi element and hopped onto its tip, as it propelled him through the stalks.

The mysterious person raced frantically ahead, its long hair flaring as its footballs stomped through the forest underbrush, with snapping twigs ringing through the air. An ice wall appeared in front of the interloper, cutting off any hope of escape. But before the thought of doubling back could enter its mind, Sung came around to confront the person.

"Stop!" he demanded.

The person cowered away and fell to its knees as a trembling voice pleaded, "Please, don't hurt me."

The fear in that voice took Sung by surprise as he stepped off the ice bridge. His right hand was at the ready to invoke his Qi elemental powers at the interloper when he saw its small frame and long black hair.

It was a teenaged girl.

Sung slowed his approach and came about her to try to see her face, but she turned further away.

"Please, please, don't hurt me," she continued to plead in her trembling voice.

"Hey, I'm not going to hurt you," said Sung soothingly. "I am Emperor Warrior Kim of the White Tiger Kingdom. Who are you?"

Her trembling stopped and she turned back cautiously. Sung was caught off guard by her wondrous eyes and angelic face. Her youthful beauty disarmed him.

The teenaged Asian girl turned and cast her eyes on the ice bridge. She turned back toward Sung and asked cautiously, "You are the White Tiger Emperor Warrior?"

Feeling confident, Sung nodded, slowly knelt down and looked at the girl staring back at him.

"Hey, I didn't mean to scare you," said Sung calmly as he continued admiring her wind-swept black hair and slender frame when he noticed that she was wearing a training outfit similar to his, underneath her white robe. He asked curiously, "Who are you?"

She furtively pulled in her white robe and looked up at Sung as she whispered, "I'm Jisoo, Park Jisoo."

Sung's eyes lit up, "You're Korean?"

Jisoo nodded slowly as she drew in her knees, almost embarrassed to be seen in such a disheveled state.

"How can that be?" asked Sung. "I thought the people that the Portal Books allowed in were the only humans on Azen."

Jisoo looked up with betrayed eyes and blurted out, "Everything the tigers have told you is a lie! I was the Empress Warrior of the White Tiger Kingdom!"

* * *

"How long have you been in this cave?" asked Sung as he looked around, which was deep within a rocky outcropping that Jisoo had led him to. The cave was quite large and was accessible only by the circuitous tunnel from which they had come. As he scanned upwards along the rocky walls, he saw many rocky ledges with small gaps along them.

Jisoo was sitting on the edge of a makeshift mattress made of straw and draped over with a white cloth. She leaned on her left side supported by her left arm, with her legs pulled inward and pressed together. With the other hand, she was stoking the small fire with a bamboo stick. The smoke rose and escaped through one of the gaps in the cave wall. Her eyes stared into the fire, but every now and then, she would look up at Sung and look away when he looked back.

"I've only been here for the past few weeks. I awoke to find myself thawing from an icy cocoon that I cast around myself to protect me," Jisoo said with dread.

"Protect you? From whom?" asked Sung.

Jisoo looked up with her piercing eyes and uttered, "From the White Tigers."

Sung was stunned. "I don't believe you."

"You have to believe me!" pleaded Jisoo. "I was summoned to Azen, for what I can imagine was many years ago. But I failed as the Empress Warrior, and the Tigeress was angry with me. They tried to send me back through the Portal Book, but it didn't accept me. I don't know why. So, I was stuck here on Azen. Fearing that I was false warrior, I was to be executed, but I escaped. But not long enough before they started to hunt me down. Though I had my Qi powers, I couldn't take on an entire army of White Tigers, and I had invoked many of the Qi powers I had left. I ran to the Origins Pool and I could hear them near me, all around me. I only had one chance. I knew that the creatures of Azen consider these pools to be sacred, so I dove into the pool. When I was near its center, I cocooned myself into the densest ice that I could create, but something went wrong. The cocoon formed, but the ice started to form inward, and before I could stop it, it froze me. I can only imagine what happened next—the cocoon of ice must have sunk to the bottom of the Origins Pool, and that's where I lay, frozen."

Sung was mesmerized by Jisoo's story, but he had a sudden realization. "But ice floats on water."

Jisoo shook her head as she responded, "Right, but something went wrong. We have far more power over ice than you realize."

Jisoo let out a sigh, and continued, "The next thing I remember, I felt water all over my face and body. The cocoon of ice around me had cracked into pieces, and I was in the water. I couldn't breathe. But I saw light above me and I instinctively reached up for it. I broke through the water and gasped for air and managed to get to the edge of the Origins Pool. I was so scared. I thought the white tigers would surely find me, with all the noise that I was making. But no one came. I was shivering and all my clothes were wet. I ran through the bamboo forest and found this cave. And I've been here ever since. I snuck out and found food and supplies by the meal prep area. I don't know how much time has passed, but if you're here, then it's at least one lunar cycle."

Jisoo looked away as she wiped away her tears.

"Hey, take your time," Sung said, attempting to assuage her sorrow.

Jisoo spun her head up toward Sung and with her deep brown eyes, she blurted out, "But you believe me, right?"

Sung paused and looked at her angelic face as his lips trembled slightly. He brushed his hand through his hair and let it stay there as he thought for a moment before he answered her. "This is just a lot. I just can't believe they would do this. Maybe we can go back to Claw Mountain…"

Before Sung could answer, she leapt up from the bed and rushed at him. Before he could step back, she grabbed him by the chest of his training top and with teary eyes, pleaded strenuously. "I can never go back there! Please, you have to believe me! We're Korean! These tigers and all the other animals are not who they seem!"

She looked deeper into Sung's eyes, and he couldn't turn away from her as she said *please* in Korean, "*Budi*!"

Sung's hands were holding her smooth hands, and he could feel the desperation in them. Despite her frantic pleadings, he couldn't ignore the beautiful scent she exuded along with her thick flowing silky hair. As he looked into her brown eyes, they suddenly turned blue and held him spellbound.

"Okay… I believe you," said Sung as a smile came across her face. She suddenly buried herself into his chest as she tenderly reached around his neck.

Sung felt awkward, but he couldn't deny how much he welcomed the warmth of her body against his. He drew her in and nestled his chin along her sensual black hair as the scent continued to intoxicate him.

Soon, she gently pushed away from him and coyly pulled the flaps of her robe over her knees as she rested her clasped hands over them. There was a coy grin on her face as she looked up at him with her icy blue yes, "You better go back, or they'll suspect something."

It took a moment for Sung to snap out of his reverie before he answered, "Yes, you're right. Why don't you stay here, and I'll come by tomorrow night with some food and water for you?"

"I would appreciate that," Jisoo said with a smile as she shifted along her knees. She was charmed by his new compassion for her.

"I have so many questions for you," said Sung as he ran his hand through his hair again.

Jisoo's voice suddenly turned melodious as she let out, "Oh, those questions don't matter. What matters is that you're here to save me."

Sung's neck flushed with warmth as he eked out a smile. "Right. Questions, who cares. All that matters is that I'm here to save you."

"Oh. You don't need to bring that silly staff with you. It didn't agree with me the last time I held it," implored Jisoo.

Sung nodded and looked about the cave and her meager dwelling. "I'll be back tomorrow, but for now, stay hidden."

Jisoo nodded, adding, "And don't forget, you can't trust the White Tigers."

Sung nodded once again and responded, "Right. I won't say a word. Okay, I'll see you tomorrow."

The smile on Jisoo's face was even more grateful as she bowed slightly, "*Gam-sa-ham-ni-da*, Emperor Warrior Kim."

Sung smiled at the tantalizing Jisoo and bowed back. He turned around and meandered through the winding tunnel. He invoked the bridge Qi element and surfed into the air just as Jisoo appeared at the entrance. With her ravenous hair flowing behind her, she watched Sung weave through the forest with her icy blue eyes.

EIGHTEEN

After a morning of manifesting more Qi elements and enjoying another lunch, the guardians led their warriors back to the Gauntlet. The warriors stood facing down the Gauntlet as the guardians came around to face them.

The Guardian Tiger stepped forward and gave the warriors a quick glance with his steely blue eyes. He rose onto his hind legs, crossed his arms and spoke. "Emperor and empress warriors, we'll be continuing your warrior pairing training today. The pairs will be Empress Warrior Wu and Emperor Warrior Nguyen on this side of the Gauntlet, and Empress Warrior Satoh and Emperor Warrior Kim, you may follow the Guardian Crane and myself to the far end."

Yuka grinned and glanced over at Sung, who shifted on his feet. He turned toward Yuka and nodded, and the two began to follow their guardians down to the far end of the Gauntlet.

"Water and wind," stated Yuka before she asked. "I wonder what we can create with that combination?"

There was no response from Sung, and she looked up curiously at him as he looked far off into the distance. She looked into the distance, and she didn't see anything that would distract him.

"Sung?" she asked?

Sung momentarily shook his head and muttered, "Oh, sorry, what?"

"What do you think we'll create with our Qi powers?" said Yuka.

"Oh, not sure, but I'm sure the guardians will tell us, and we'll figure it out," said Sung dismissively.

"I guess so," answered Yuka.

The guardians came to a stop and turned toward their warriors. The Guardian Crane addressed them, "Empress and emperor warriors, for your first pairing, let's do something easy. Ice wall and wind."

As the guardians walked off to the side, Sung turned to Yuka blankly.

Yuka nodded her head quickly and suggested, "How about you create a tall ice wall and I'll knock it down?"

Sung nodded and stepped back as Yuka walked off to the side. Sung magnetically slapped his staff onto this back and he invoked the wall Qi element. A short and squat ice wall appeared about fifty feet away from them.

Yuka gave him a confused look and said, "It's too short and wide, I won't be able to knock that down. Can you make it tall and thin?"

"Ah, oh right," said Sung in an apologetic tone. He evaporated the squat wall with a quick invocation. With his jittery fingers, he brushed out the Korean word for wall, but it didn't conjure up. With a look of frustration, he brushed out the Korean word for wall again, and with a clench and quick flick of his hand, he invoked a taller and slender ice wall. It glistened in the sun when the ice wall abruptly started to sway before it fell over and shattered upon impact.

"Man! What the hell!" said Sung as he brought his hands to his knees and looked at the shattered ice.

"Are you okay?" asked Yuka. "You don't seem like yourself today."

"I'm sorry," said Sung as he paused before he continued. "I didn't get a good night's sleep, so I'm a bit tired."

Yuka nodded in understanding before the Guardian Tiger approached.

"Emperor Warrior Kim, is everything all right?" he asked firmly.

"I'm sorry, Guardian Tiger," said Sung. "I… I didn't get a good night's sleep, so I'm not fully myself today. I won't do it again."

"Very well. I would recommend taking a deep breath and focusing," said the Guardian Tiger.

Sung nodded and the Guardian Tiger walked away. When he reached the onlooking Guardian Crane, Sung evaporated the shattered ice and looked up at Yuka.

"Let's try again," he said as he rubbed his hands together.

"Mmm," Yuka elicited as she nodded and stepped away.

Sung looked focused as he exhaled. He closed his eyes and when he reopened them, he invoked another ice wall that was about twenty feet high, five feet in length, and two feet wide.

Yuka smiled as she soared into the air and invoked the gust Qi element and directed it at the upper portion of the ice wall. Upon impact, the wall tipped away from her and crashed onto the ground with a thud as it broke into large ice chunks.

While in the air, Yuka gave the thumbs up and hollered, "Create ten more! Let me practice knocking them over."

"Like dominoes!" said Sung as he went ahead and conjured up more ice walls that Yuka effortlessly knocked down.

They continued practicing, and despite getting the pair of Qi elements working together, Yuka still felt that Sung seemed off. On their next Qi pairing, Yuka invoked an open cube of air made of air walls, which Sung filled with water. But he constantly overfilled it or in one instance, filled it with ice. Yuka chided him, "If I release the walls of air, it'll just be a block of ice."

Sung shook his head in frustration, and they continued their pair training well into the late afternoon until it was time for dinner. During dinner, Clara and Daniel chatted about the fire sinkholes that they created along with the other Qi pairings. When Yuka excitedly talked about the ice walls that she toppled over, she saw that Sung seemed detached from the conversation. She noticed that he made several glances toward the food prep area. She didn't share how he made some clumsy Qi elements to spare him the embarrassment, but she knew that something was off with Sung that day.

Afterwards, the warriors returned to their tent quarters, but Yuka couldn't keep Sung out of her mind as she laid on her side underneath the soft quilt blanket. Though he eventually invoked the water Qi elements properly, she was concerned that their pairing hadn't been successful. Come battle time, if they were off, it could be deadly.

She gingerly got out of bed, changed out of her sleepwear and into her training attire. She picked up the moon star from the end table and fastened it at her waist. Her feet pattered across the tatami mats and slipped into her boots. After pushing back the thick tent flap, she walked into the cool night. A few cranes nodded at her as she made her way to Sung's tent quarters.

As she walked toward the White Tiger area, a few tigers respectfully greeted her, and she did the same. As she came upon Sung's tent, all was quiet.

"Sung," Yuka called out, but there was no answer. She wondered where he was and gently pulled back the flap to the tent's entrance. As she entered cautiously, she called once more, "Sung?"

But an empty tent greeted her. She looked around until her eyes fell upon the Claw Staff lying on the bed. Her eyes widened and she wondered where he could be without his staff. She spun around and upon exiting the tent, she came upon a white tiger who looked at her.

"Empress Warrior Satoh," it spoke.

"Good evening," said Yuka nervously before she asked, "Do you know where Sung is?"

The white tiger's eyebrow rose momentarily before it turned his massive head in the direction of the food prep area. Yuka nodded, relieved that Sung was only getting a bite to eat. He didn't seem to eat much during dinner, as she recalled.

As the white tiger walked away, Yuka invoked the fly Qi element and flew into the night sky toward the food prep area. She made it there in no time and from above, the food prep area was bathed in light from the illumination jades. She saw some panda kitchen attendants milling about, but there was no sign of Sung.

As she hovered silently, wondering where he may be, she caught movement along a path and squinted at it. It was Sung, hurrying along the path. Yuka cocked her head and silently flew through the sky, keeping her eyes on Sung from above. She saw him furtively looking back. There was something in his hand, but before she could see what it was, he invoked an ice bridge and surfed along its tip. Yuka stayed out of his line of sight and easily followed the ice bridge when suddenly, it vanished. Her eyes lit up in alarm, but she looked up ahead and saw that the path led to the Origins Pool.

Perhaps he had wanted to see his mother or father? But how could he if he didn't have his Claw Staff? she wondered. She didn't ponder too long as she flew through the air and carefully landed on the edge of the bamboo line surrounding the Origins Pool. She invoked her fly Qi element but adjusted it, allowing her to skim mere inches above the ground. She quickly made her way to the Origins Pool, and when she reached it, she slowed her approach to avoid detection.

But there was no sign of Sung by the Origins Pool. She scanned the area and became worried when she heard a twig snap. She quickly floated toward the noise and saw Sung from behind, walking some distance up ahead. Her curiosity was piqued as she floated through the bamboo stalks, trying to stay silent. He walked some distance before he came to a cave entrance that was partially hidden by the roots of a large tree growing above. Just as he was about to enter, Yuka floated right up behind him and whispered sharply, "Sung!"

Sung jolted into the air and spun around as his eyes popped in surprise.

"Yuka!" he said under his breath as he looked left and right before he walked towards her. "What are you doing here?"

"I was going to ask you the same," said Yuka.

"You can't be here," he said urgently as he gently ushered her back and away from the cave entrance.

"Why not?" asked the Yuka. "And who's the food for?"

Sung looked very frazzled and said dismissively, "It's not for anyone. It's for me."

"I don't believe you. Why would you come to a cave to eat?" she asked firmly.

Sung looked down knowing that his ruse was not believable. "Okay, if I tell you, you promise not to tell anyone."

Yuka looked at him and nodded without promising him.

"Okay, so you know, I don't think the guardians have been truthful with us. I know this because... because I met another empress warrior," said Sung.

Yuka's expression went blank. "What are you talking about?"

"Shhhhh," said Sung. "She's a previous empress warrior, she's Korean. Her name is Jisoo and what a cutie! She has been trapped here since the last cycle. She was cast out by the white tigers long ago and they were going to kill her. But somehow, her Qi elemental power froze her in an icy cocoon within the Origins Pool, and it only recently cracked open, allowing her to escape. I came across her last night and she told me all of this. I don't think the guardians have been truthful."

Yuka looked at Sung in disbelief before she said, "That can't be true. The guardians have trained us and treated us well…"

"Yes, to fight their battles," said Sung. "And what happens if we fail? What do they do to failed warriors?"

Yuka was silent but she continued to ask, "Well where is she from? How has she been surviving all alone by herself all this time? What happened to the other warriors during…"

Sung shook his head vigorously to silence her, "I don't have all the answers, but let me talk to her and get more answers. Once I learn more, I will tell you, Clara, and Daniel, and we can decide what to do."

"Can I meet her?" asked Yuka.

"No, she was very scared and right now, I'm the only one she trusts," said Sung.

"I don't like this," said a skeptical Yuka.

"Don't worry. She's harmless, but if she's a former Azen warrior, we need to help her. Promise me you won't tell anyone else," Sung pleaded.

Yuka grudgingly nodded but kept her eyes on Sung's eyes. She saw a sense of urgency in them.

"Thanks. Trust me. She's one of us," assuaged Sung. "As soon as I know more, I'll come by your quarters tonight. Okay?"

"Okay," said Yuka as she brought her cool hands together and wrestled with her own misgivings. She wanted to trust Sung, but something was wrong. Though her intuition was telling her so, she didn't let on.

Sung smiled, "Okay, why don't you go back to your tent, and I'll find you later tonight?"

"Okay," said Yuka softly as she took a few steps back. As she walked toward the bamboo stalks, she turned back to see Sung disappear into the cave entrance. She quickly invoked the fly Qi element and skillfully flew her way out of the stalks. When she came to the Origins Pool, she soared upward and toward the tent complex.

* * *

Yuka landed with a thud in front of Clara's tent and burst through the entrance. "Clara!" she blurted out just as Clara was about to change out of her training attire. Clara was startled as she pulled the flap of her training top across her chest. She gazed at an anxious Yuka.

Yuka barged in and stepped onto the tatami floor mats as Clara suddenly pointed at Yuka's boots. Yuka stopped in mid-step and brushed away Clara's concern and interjected, "I think Sung is in trouble!"

As they sat on the end of the bed, Yuka looked flustered. She summarized her encounter with Sung and his mysterious encounter with a previous warrior who was hiding from the white tigers. Suddenly, Yuka didn't know who to trust, her friends or the guardians.

Clara stared into Yuka's anxious eyes and said, "We need to tell my guardian."

"But I told Sung that I wouldn't tell them," said Yuka.

"But I didn't," said Clara. "Come on!"

After grabbing the Bow of Destiny and quiver and slipping into her boots, Clara and Yuka bolted out of the tent. They ran toward the Guardian Panda's tent and dispensing with the formalities, they barged in.

"Guardian Panda!" exclaimed Clara with Yuka behind her. "I'm sorry to disturb you, but it's urgent."

The Guardian Panda was in a chair carved from a large section of bamboo with a scroll in his hand as he looked up. His eyes widened at the sudden intrusion, but he collected himself as he spoke. "Empress Warriors Wu and Satoh, what's the matter?"

"It's Sung," said Clara hurriedly. "Yuka can tell you."

When Yuka quickly recapped her encounter with Sung, the Guardian Panda's eyes lit up as he blurted out, "*Huli jing!*"

Clara mouthed the Chinese word that she never heard of, "*Huli jing?*"

"Yes!" said the Guardian Panda as he leapt off his chair. "We must hurry," he urged.

"What is a *huli jing*?" asked Clara as the Guardian Panda walked by her and Yuka.

"It is a shapeshifter," said the Guardian Panda.

"A shapeshifter?" asked Yuka.

"In Japanese, they are called *bakemono*.

Yuka's eyes widened and she gasped as the Guardian Panda reached for his staff.

"What's a *bakemono*?" asked Clara as she suddenly felt tension fill the air.

Yuka turned toward Clara, "They are shapeshifters who usually take the form of a beautiful woman to lure men and do horrible things to them. But I thought they weren't real."

As the Guardian Panda raced toward the tent entrance with Clara and Yuka quickly following, he exclaimed, "They are real here on Azen! We must gather the other guardians or Sung may be doomed!"

NINETEEN

"It's up ahead," Yuka said urgently as she led the way through the bamboo stalks, followed by Clara, the Guardian Panda, and Tiger. Behind them, several battle pandas and tigers carried jade torches to light the way. The cranes that ferried them took up the rear, but the Guardian Crane and Buffalo were absent, since the Guardian Panda didn't have time to summon them.

"There!" Yuka hollered as she pointed to the half-hidden cave entrance.

"Empress Warriors Wu and Satoh, ready your weapons!" said the Guardian Panda as he and the Guardian Tiger pushed forward. The Guardian Tiger bared his claws and snarled as he took up the rear as Yuka entered, with Clara trailing her with the Guardian Panda close behind. The jade torches cast eerie shadows along the rocky walls. It was narrow, making it difficult for the guardians to move through it unencumbered. The cranes were too large to enter the cave entrance, so they stood guard as the battle pandas and tigers dashed into the cave.

Yuka moved about the damp, winding tunnel for some distance before it opened up into a small cavern. Her eyes lit up and she gasped as Clara came up from behind.

"Sung!" screamed Yuka as she watched him lying face up across the lap of a strange young girl. Her voluminous black hair was thrown over her shoulder as she was deeply kissing him. She glanced up suddenly as blue wisps floated upwards from Sung's mouth, revealing her icy blue eyes. Yuka and Clara jolted backwards and into the Guardian Panda and Tiger, who finally got through the tight cave tunnel.

"*Gumiho!*" the Guardian Tiger uttered as the Guardian Panda let out, "*Huli jing!*"

She pulled her hand away from the back of Sung's neck as his listless head fell back onto her knees. His eyes were closed, and his mouth was slightly open as the *gumiho* slid her hand down to his chest and rubbed it.

Her expression showed annoyance and defiance as she screamed out, "You are too late! He's gone!"

She quickly pressed her lips onto Sung's and inhaled with all her might as his arms went limp.

"Warriors! Destroy her before it's too late!" commanded the Guardian Panda as the Guardian Tiger moved around him.

Yuka whipped off a moon star while Clara released a jade-tipped arrow. But before they could sink themselves into the *gumiho*, she vanished in a puff of smoke as a moon star and arrow passed right through. When the smoke settled, in its wake was a sensual woman with Asian features, her ravenous black hair flowing, glistening in a white robe. But what stood out were the nine furry tails that unfurled behind her. The conniving nine-tailed fox had made her appearance.

The Guardian Tiger leapt at her, but she vanished into smoke once again as Sung's unresponsive head hit the ground with a light thud, tilting toward his fellow warriors.

"Sung!" said Yuka as she raced over with Clara.

Two other battle tigers sprang forward, their eyes darting about the cavern, which was illuminated by a small fire, when the Guardian Tiger pointed upward and roared. Casting their jade torches upward, they saw perched on top of the ledge a small white fox with pristine fur and nine fluffy tails. The fox's icy blue eyes stared down at the assortment of rescuers as she took delight in her trickery. When the tigers sprang upward toward her, she smiled, ducked into a gap in the rocky wall, and disappeared.

Yuka reached Sung and gently lifted his head into her lap. She brushed back his hair as Clara knelt by his side. The Guardian Panda came up behind her and looked down at Sung's motionless body.

"Sung!" screamed Yuka. "Wake up! Please!"

Clara's face was contorted as she placed her hand on Sung's chest, "Sung! Wake up!"

"It's not a mortal wound," uttered the Guardian Panda as the Guardian Tiger came up behind him. His eyes bulged at the sight of the fallen emperor warrior that he was sworn to protect.

"He won't wake up!" said Yuka.

The Guardian Panda shot a look at Clara and curtly said, "Empress Warrior Wu, you need to bring him back to life!"

Clara looked up, "What?"

"You, you need to bring him back to life as only you can!"

"Like how, with CPR?" Her eyes became blurry and confused.

"No, you are the earth Wu. You command the Qi of life. You can replenish it. You can give it life once more, but we must hurry."

Clara shook her head in confusion and looked up, "How?"

The Guardian Panda scurried around Sung's legs and knelt across from Clara. Yuka continued holding his head, only able to watch what was going on.

"But we haven't trained her yet," protested the Guardian Tiger, who also settled onto his haunches.

"She will have to learn now!" declared the Guardian Panda.

The Guardian Panda looked at Clara sternly and said, "Keep your hand on his chest and place your other hand on top."

With her unsure hands on Sung's chest, she looked up at the Guardian Panda and asked, "Okay, now what?"

"You are the earth Wu. You can feel the Qi within you, but you can also send it into another living being whose Qi may have been depleted."

Clara was confused. "What?"

"Trust me. Trust what I am about to say to you and trust your instinct," implored the Guardian Panda. "Relax and breathe, yes, that's it. Now close your eyes and reach deep within yourself to feel your own Qi. You know it's there."

Clara nodded as the tears that had streamed down her face dried up. She exhaled and tried to feel what was still new to her. But all she felt was Sung's still chest with no heartbeat, and she panicked. "I can't! Sung can't be dead!"

The Guardian Panda's voice sliced through the air, "Empress Warrior Wu, concentrate! Feel your Qi, that inner warmth that is your lifeforce."

Clara nodded and exhaled as she repositioned her hands on Sung's chest.

"You can do it, Clara," Yuka said encouragingly.

Clara pressed a bit harder onto Sung's chest and focused. She cleared out her mind and saw inward. She listened to her heartbeat and soon, she connected with it. She could feel its warmth and how it pushed out a nourishing warmth throughout her body. It was steady, and she could feel it.

"You can feel it now?" asked the Guardian Panda, to which she nodded. "Good, now feel your Qi, embrace it, and channel it through your arms, into your hands, and into Emperor Warrior Kim."

Clara nodded silently. Her eyes closed as she focused on her breathing. She felt the warmth in her chest and followed it through her arms. But she felt more this time: She could hone in on her Qi coursing throughout her body. Her mind traveled to her palms and down to Sung's lukewarm chest as she pressed harder. Clara inhaled deeply. To Yuka's amazement, she saw a slithering green glow travel from Clara's shoulders down her arms, into her hands, and finally into Sung's chest. The entanglement of Qi started to weave outward and soon, the glowing tendrils of Qi could be seen under his top. The glow grew brighter until it seeped into Sung's chest all at once. Sung's eyes bolted open as he let out a gasp. He brought his hands to his chest, then clasped Clara's hands. He first looked upward at Yuka before turning to Clara.

"Sung! You're alive!" screamed Yuka as Clara let out a sigh of relief. She smiled and gently pulled her hands off Sung's chest and gently held his hands.

"What, what happened?" Sung muttered out loud as he struggled to take in another breath.

Clara looked up at the Guardian Tiger, who let out a thankful sigh. She looked up at the Guardian Panda, who simply said, "Well done."

Clara nodded with a relieved grin as the Guardian Tiger said, "Thank you, Empress Warrior Wu. I am grateful to you."

As Sung struggled to lean upwards from his supine position, Yuka supported him as he mumbled, "What just happened?"

Clara couldn't help chuckling under her breath as Yuka blurted out, "You were seduced by a nine-tailed fox!"

TWENTY

Sung could hear incoherent mumbling. He felt warmth on his body, most likely from the sun. But his mind was in a daze, and he tried to shake it off. His eyes fluttered open, and the indistinct shapes started to come into focus.

"Sung!" he heard someone say.

He turned to the voice, and Yuka's face came into focus as she sat along the right edge of his bed at Claw Mountain. He brought his hand up to ward off the morning sun as he squinted.

"Hey," Sung said hesitantly as he swiveled his head. He could see Clara, Daniel, and all the guardians. "What's going on?"

"You are safe, Emperor Warrior Kim," said the Guardian Tiger, who came up to Sung's bedside. Sung looked into his large blue eyes as his massive white-and-black striped fur face came into view. He could feel the Guardian Tiger's presence along with his hot breath.

"Man," said Sung bashfully. "All I can remember was this girl that I was trying to save. She said she was a former empress warrior."

"A lie," said the Guardian Tiger. "She was a *gumiho*. The conniving nine-tailed fox that usually takes the form of a beautiful young woman to seduce young men. That is how she is known in Korean. In Chinese, she is known as the *huli jing*, in Japanese, she is known as…"

"*Kitsune!*" Yuka blurted out as the Guardian Tiger looked at her and nodded.

"Yes, *kitsune*. The Warlock employs these mystical creatures to sabotage our efforts. They belong to a class of creatures that Yuka would refer to as *bakemono*, or shapeshifters. But in the *gumiho's* case, she is a nine-tailed fox that can shape shift into a beautiful young woman to prey on unsuspecting young men. In this case, you."

Sung closed his eyes and reopened them as he looked upwards, "Man, I feel so dumb."

"Do not feel ashamed, Emperor Warrior Kim," said the Guardian Tiger.

"The *gumiho* is cunning and is a master of seduction and bringing young men under her spell, either to manipulate them or to siphon off their Qi. In your case, it was the latter, and she almost succeeded."

Sung struggled slightly to get up, and Yuka gently propped up another pillow behind his head. "Siphon off my Qi? Did she succeed?"

"She may or may not have," said the Guardian Tiger. "We may never know. But if we didn't arrive when we did, it may have been too late."

"Was... was I dead?" asked Sung.

"Almost," said the Guardian Tiger gravely. "Your Qi had just been siphoned off when we arrived, and luckily, we arrived at that instant. If not, we would have lost you."

"But how... how was I brought back to life?" asked Sung.

"Empress Warrior Wu," said the Guardian Panda as the Guardian Tiger's furry face and blue eyes glanced up at him. "She brought you back to life. As the wielder of the earth Wu element, she has the ability to replenish another being's Qi."

Sung looked at Clara as she smiled and waved awkwardly. He nodded in her direction and humbly said, "Thanks."

"Luckily," said the Guardian Tiger. "The Guardian Panda was able to help her invoke her power and bring you back. We had not taught her this power yet, but she was able to invoke it intuitively."

Sung nodded as he contemplated. "So, everything with Jisoo, it's all a bit foggy—was a lie?"

"All of it," answered the Guardian Tiger firmly.

"So, there aren't former warriors who are outcasts?"

"No, there are not."

"So, all warriors eventually go back home through the Portal Books?" asked Sung.

There was a pause and the Guardian Panda interjected, "Yes." The

Guardian Panda then furtively made eye contact with the Guardian Tiger, who nodded.

"Oh man," said Sung. "I feel like such a fool."

"There is no reason to feel that way," said the Guardian Tiger. "We haven't had the time to explain all the details of Azen to all of you. That is why it's important for all of you to carry your jaded weapons with you at all times. The jade helps to ward off these mystical creatures. So, warriors, please keep your weapons close to you at all times."

The warriors nodded as Clara instinctively looked down at the Bamboo Jade embedded in her bow.

"We should let you rest, Emperor Warrior Kim," said the Guardian Panda as he motioned toward all the other guardians.

"Rest well with your fellow warriors," said the Guardian Tiger as he rested his large furry paw on top of Sung's left hand. Sung was taken aback by the affection of his guardian and smiled back.

The Guardian Tiger nodded and withdrew his paw and started to turn away. The remaining guardians nodded in Sung's direction as they left the room, leaving only the warriors. Clara sat down on the edge of the bed behind Yuka as Daniel walked to the corner of the bed.

"Wow, I can't believe that happened," said Sung.

"Dude!" said Daniel excitedly. "You were seduced by Ahri!"

Everyone looked up at Daniel with a vexed expression as Sung exclaimed, "Ahri?"

"You know! The nine-tailed fox character from League of Legends!" said Daniel.

"Who?" asked Sung.

"Dude, you're playing way too much StarCraft. You need to play League of Legends when you get back."

"Um, okay," said Sung.

"Was she hot?" asked Daniel.

Sung looked up at Daniel dumbfounded and asked, "What?"

"You know, was she… hot?" asked Daniel curiously.

Sung turned his head and looked upwards as memories of Jisoo replayed in his mind and a smile spread across his face. "Oh man, was she! Wow, she had this thick flowing hair. Her blue eyes were amazing, it was like you could fall into them. Her face was so smooth and her lips, were like so red and luscious…"

"Dude… you're turning red," said Daniel.

Sung shot a surprised look at Daniel and stammered, "No I'm not!"

"Dude you are!" taunted Daniel with a big smile.

Yuka and Clara looked at Sung and saw that his cheeks were flushed and were getting even redder. They looked at each other and giggled at Sung's embarrassment. Sung brought his hands up to his cheeks and he couldn't deny it, his cheeks were warm.

Sung pulled one of the pillows from beneath his head and placed it over his face as he mumbled something incoherent into it.

"Yep, she was hot," said Daniel confidently.

TWENTY - ONE

Sung focused his eyes on his brush strokes. Each one was deliberate and perfect as he manifested more Qi elements from the Portal Book. He was determined to manifest as many as possible in anticipation of the next battle. Revenge was on his mind, and he still felt embarrassed to have been seduced by Jisoo, the *gumiho*. Though he knew his friends didn't blame him, he was wrestling with his own conflicted thoughts and wasn't yet ready to face his friends.

They had finished dinner earlier, and everyone else was also focused on manifesting. Everyone knew that they needed to add to their arsenal of Qi elemental powers. He remembered he came close to depleting his icicles in the first battle, and he wanted to be sure he wasn't going to be in the same vulnerable situation.

Sung's eyes looked up as he saw that the four guardians were approaching. He sighed and allowed a final manifested Qi element to seep into his chest. He propped the Clawdium brush back on top of the book and stepped back from the Portal Book. He looked around and saw everyone else doing the same. Daniel nodded at him, and he nodded back. He looked up into the sky and saw that the next moon was almost in position.

"Emperor Warrior Kim," greeted the Guardian Tiger as he took his spot across the Portal Book from Sung.

"Guardian Tiger," said Sung somberly. "Is it almost time?"

The Guardian Tiger nodded as the Guardian Crane got into her position. He nodded at Sung and walked around him and entered the center of the Portal Circle.

"Emperor and empress warriors," said the Guardian Tiger firmly as his massive white and black striped frame circled about the center. "The next lunar eclipse of the moon is almost upon us. Like before, it will only last a few minutes, so let's observe it. We call this moon *Ngoc Trai*."

Daniel's ears perked up upon hearing the Guardian Tiger speak a Vietnamese word. He looked puzzled and turned toward the Guardian Buffalo who spoke, "That is the word for pearl in Vietnamese."

Daniel nodded as he whispered *ngoc trai* to himself a few times before looking up at the moon.

Clara glanced over at Sung, and saw that he was already looking up. She noticed that he had been a bit withdrawn and engrossed in manifestation. She admired his lean stature, a trait befitting a young warrior. She twisted about and saw that her Guardian Panda was looking up. She exhaled and looked up with him.

Ngoc Trai was beautiful with its tint of blue and green. A shadow had already started to creep up on the moon, and she watched in nervous anticipation. The whole lunar eclipse would be captivating if it didn't portend forthcoming evil. Soon, the entire Portal Circle grew darker as everyone's silhouettes blended into the night shadows. Only the whites of their eyes continued to glow, but it was the steely blue eyes of the Guardian Tiger that caught her attention as they seemed to float in the darkness.

Soon, the drape of darkness started to peel back as moonlight brightened up the surroundings. The lunar eclipse was over.

The Guardian Tiger re-entered the Portal Circle and announced, "It's done. The Warlock's second army has landed. The scouts will tell us which direction they will be coming from, north, south, or west."

Clara raised her hand and the Guardian Tiger's bright catlike eyes focused in on her. "Yes, Empress Warrior Wu?"

"How are these spots chosen by the Warlock?" asked Clara.

The Guardian Tiger nodded and got up onto his hind legs, pushing himself into a standing position. He reached out with his right paw, and fiery tendrils wove out from the water Wu Portal Book. They danced around him, encircling him before forming the kingdoms of Azen.

"The kingdoms, except the Crane Kingdom, are all within a continuous piece of land, which is Azen," explained the Guardian Tiger. "To the east and west of Azen, we are buttressed by an impassable glassy terrain that is broken by deep fissures and crevasses. This is the Shards. This is what separates us from Nadi, the Warlock's land. It is not passable on foot, by us or even the Warlock's demon creatures. Only the forces of the Crane Kingdom may fly over it. To the north and south are the great oceans. Along the northern, western, southern and eastern most points of Azen, are four distinct areas."

"For some unknown reason, before documented time, the Warlock became able to teleport his newly spawned army during each lunar eclipse to these points. Over thousands of years, it was observed that he cannot choose the same spot during the same lunar cycle. But in an off-lunar cycle when the fifth moon enters its lunar eclipse, the Warlock has an additional chance to teleport his army to any cardinal point that he chooses."

"Many generations ago, during the lull in between lunar cycles, we have looked to see if there was something in any of the three earthen spots that controlled the Warlock's ability to teleport his demon army. But we found nothing. We could not explore the northern spot as it is a watery point. But knowing what to expect, we can anticipate and prepare. Are there any additional questions?"

Daniel's voice caused the Guardian Tiger to prowl about as he attuned his ears. "Where does the Warlock spawn his evil creatures?" Daniel asked.

The ears of the Guardian Tiger fluttered as he pawed the glowing tendrils that shaped the terrain of Azen. The entire landscape shifted westward, crossing over the jagged Shards until a large stone fortress sitting high above on a mountain top appeared. Its image wasn't as sharp as the other structures in Azen, but it looked ominous.

"We believe," the Guardian Tiger explained, "that somewhere within the fortress is where the Warlock spawns his demon armies. We don't have any more information than that, as we have never been inside of it. What information that we do have has been gleaned from stealthy missions led by the cranes in the past."

Yuka raised her hand, and the Guardian Tiger turned to her and nodded.

"What lies beyond the Warlock's fortress?" Yuka asked.

The Guardian Tiger's left eyebrow raised momentarily and answered, "We do not know. The cranes have never ventured further than that."

Clara raised her hand, and the Guardian Tiger turned to her.

"So, what do we do now?" she asked. She could feel anxiety stirring in the pit of her stomach.

"What we have always done," answered the Guardian Tiger. "Continue manifesting and soon, we will know which direction we will need to head toward. Then we march."

Clara nodded and glanced quickly at her fellow warriors.

"Very well then," the Guardian Tiger began. "As you were. Your fellow guardians and I need to work with our kingdom armies before the march."

"Yes, Guardian Tiger," the warriors said in unison before they turned back to their Portal Books to continue manifesting.

* * *

Lunch the next day was somewhat subdued, as the guardians were still with their respective armies and only the warriors were eating. The tension was high all around.

"How's your hand?" Sung asked the others.

"A little stiff, to be honest," said Clara.

"I've never written so many Japanese characters before," said Yuka as she rubbed her right hand with her left.

"I've never even written so much Vietnamese until I came to Azen," Daniel whined.

There was a moment of silence before everyone let out a soft laugh.

"We'll be ready," said Clara confidently. "Look at how well we did the first time around."

Daniel nodded and smirked, "Not too bad for a half Asian."

"Not too bad at all for an Asian, bro," chided Sung with a smile before he fist-bumped Daniel, who smiled back appreciatively.

"They're back," said Yuka as her eyes perked up upon seeing the guardians approaching.

Everyone put down their chopsticks, wiped their hands, and turned to the guardians as they approached the edge of the table.

"West," said the Guardian Tiger firmly. "They have arrived in the west, and it is a three-days' march for them. The western point is guarded by a magnificently strong gate that the White Tiger Kingdom built long ago. It has never been breached. We will be traveling to *Seodaemun* in the morning."

Sung raised his hand, and the Guardian Tiger nodded. "Do we know what type of creature we will be fighting this time?" he asked.

"They seem to be of the *nue* type," said the Guardian Tiger. "They are agile and ferocious creatures. Even more cunning that the *Huo Dou* Demon Fire Dogs."

"Oh great," muttered Clara under her breath.

"The *nue* is an abomination," the Guardian Tiger continued. "It has the head of a monkey, the torso of a tiger, and the tail of a venomous snake. It is agile, ferocious like a demonic monkey with a tail that has a mind of its own that you need to keep an eye out for. A formidable adversary, but one that we are familiar with."

The warriors nodded as the Guardian Tiger said, "Emperor and empress warriors, continue to manifest and arm yourself with your Qi elemental powers. Get a good night's rest, and we will come get you in the morning."

"Yes, Guardian Tiger," said the warriors in unison as the guardians left the Portal Circle.

* * *

The next morning, Clara was calm, but she could feel the tension. She was wearing a fresh set of training gear and pulled everything taut against her body. She eyed the bamboo wardrobe holding her battle armor, which had been delivered to her tent quarters earlier for a last-minute fitting. She walked over to her battle wardrobe with anticipation. With her hands on its handles, she let out a breath and opened it to reveal her impressive battle armor. She smiled as she admired its light gray chest plate and how the green jade dust swirled along the body contours. Her eyes glided over the shoulder guards, the gauntlets for her forearms, the magnetic thigh armor plates, and finally, the awesome boots. Her eyes fell upon the helmet that sat in between the boots and admired the white panda logo that emerged from the light green jade dust that flared along the top. She was looking forward to donning it once more. It made her feel like a superhero.

The sound of the flap to her tent caught her attention, and she carefully closed the wardrobe as the Guardian Panda entered.

"Good morning, Empress Warrior Wu," said the Guardian Panda as he nodded toward Clara.

Clara also nodded and responded, "Good morning, Guardian Panda."

Her eyes peeked over as two more panda attendants entered the room.

"They will be taking your battle wardrobe to the battle front," said the Guardian Panda. "Are you ready for the march?"

Clara turned to pick up the Bow of Destiny and its quiver. She slung them about her body, looked at the Guardian Panda, and said, "Ready."

Clara followed the Guardian Panda out of the tent until they reached the staging point. She strode up the slight incline toward her fellow warriors, whose backs were turned to her. As she approached, Yuka heard her footsteps, turned around, and waved gently to her.

"Morning," said Clara.

"As good as any morning before a battle," said Daniel casually.

"Yah, not too many high schoolers can say that, I bet," said Sung.

They let out a chuckle as Sung and Daniel gave Clara some space between them. She cast her eye out and she could see the kingdom armies amassing, organizing into orderly formations. The cranes were up in front inspecting their katana wings. The water buffalos were securing their battle armor while the tigers were stretching in their meshed bodysuit armor. The battle pandas took up the rear, checking the fit of their bamboo armor as each embedded green jade faintly glowed. The chariots and wagons were filled with armaments, emplacements, and other equipment.

"It's just like last time," said Yuka. "I'll be flying ahead of you with all the cranes. I heard that a regiment of tigers were already flown out earlier on the backs of the eagles to man the gate. Sung and Daniel will march with their tiger and buffalo armies, and Clara will take up the rear with all the pandas and the supplies."

"Seems very orderly," said Clara as she looked at everyone. She took a step back allowing all of them to fall into a tight circle. She looked up at everyone and all eyes fell on her. She brought up her clenched fists to her chest, the back of her hands facing out and elbows at the side. Sung, Yuka and Daniel did the same.

"For Azen!" they all said firmly in unison.

"To *Seodaemun*!" said Sung with pride.

TWENTY - TWO

"I think we're close," said Sung wearily as he rode atop the Guardian Tiger.

"Maybe it's beyond that bend," remarked Daniel.

"We are almost there, Emperor Warrior Kim and Nguyen," said the Guardian Tiger's voice from beneath them. "Emperor Warrior Nguyen is right, *Seodaemun* is around the bend."

"Finally!" said Sung. He quickly added, "Not that I don't mind riding on your back for the past few hours."

"It is my pleasure, Emperor Warrior Kim," said the Guardian Tiger. "What effort is there in carrying one human?"

Sung smiled, lifting his gaze as the Guardian Tiger's muscular body rounded the bend. His eyes widened as he saw what loomed ahead: the great western gate of *Seodaemun* of Azen. It had all the architectural styling of the Korean gates that he had seen in pictures. The gate had the expected sloped roof, but its size stood out. It was also wide and straddled a high, white stone wall. An additional roofed structure stood on either side of the main structure. In the middle of the stone wall, he could barely make out the top of the stone arched tunnel entrance, which was obscured by the bustling of the armies settling in.

"Impressed?" asked the Guardian Tiger.

"Am I!" said Sung in wonder as his eyes continued to fixate on the roofed structures atop the gate. "What's making the roof shine like that?"

"Clawdium," said the Guardian Tiger. "The roof tiles are of pure Clawdium."

"Whoa," said Sung. "It's even bigger than the ones back in Korea."

"We've had generations to perfect it," said the Guardian Tiger.

"Gotcha," said Sung. "Dude, are you seeing this?"

"Uh-huh," said Daniel, impressed with the size of the wall. "It's so big, but we're still so far away. And it's never been breached?"

"No, it has not," replied the Guardian Tiger. "But many generations ago, the blood of our ancestors was spilled here to protect the Portal Books. The sacrifice was so great many generations ago that the great Tigeror of that time commissioned the great western wall to be built. Unlike the choke point of Jagged Pass, which has a natural defense, this span between the mountain edges is too great to be easily defendable. In one lunar cycle, only the wall was built, and it held through the next battle. In the next lunar cycle lull after that, the wall was thickened and larger stones were quarried. Our great friends the water buffalos were instrumental in assisting us in transporting the larger stones."

"I've heard those stories of long ago as well," said the Guardian Buffalo soulfully.

The Guardian Tiger nodded and continued, "Once the wall was fortified, its height brought it to its true glory and the battle chambers within the wall were completed, with the battle fortresses built on top. The first one was built of pristine bamboo, but in the next battle, the entire structure almost burnt to the ground. But the gate held. In the next cycle lull, new fortresses were built, but instead of only bamboo, Clawdium was used. It was an immense undertaking to mine that much Clawdium. But mine they did, and the fortresses, fortified with Clawdium, have stood since."

"Wow," Sung let out. "How many soldiers can stand on the gate?"

"Maybe a thousand," said the Guardian Tiger cautiously.

"Whoa!" said Sung. "That's intense."

"Guardian Tiger?" asked Daniel respectfully.

"Yes, Emperor Warrior Nguyen?" the Guardian Tiger responded as he tilted his head upward toward Daniel.

"As big as the gate is, isn't the tunnel itself the weakest point?" asked Daniel.

The Guardian Tiger smiled and spoke. "The outer tunnel is protected by heavy swinging doors, whose width is as long as the length of one bamboo staff. They are made of pure Clawdium. Within the arched tunnel are two additional walls that slide into place, and those are also made of pure Clawdium. Their width is as long as one bamboo section. And on the inner opening of the arched tunnel is yet another set of heavy swinging doors that is again, the width of the length of one bamboo staff: That too is made of pure Clawdium. The outer door has never been breached, and should they breach it, the entire floor of the arched tunnel retracts. Below that is a steep drop with Clawdium spikes embedded into the ground."

"Way cool," said Daniel as he envisioned the devious defenses of the western gate and its tunneled archway.

"We have arrived," said the Guardian Tiger as the Guardian Buffalo followed him to the side, allowing the regiments of tigers and buffalos to pass by. Tent quarters were being set up at the back of the land that led to the western gate, which was still at least a thousand feet away.

Sung and Daniel climbed down from their guardians and fidgeted with their weapons as both of their guardians returned to upright positions and stretched out their backs.

A shadow soon cast itself over Sung and Daniel, causing them to look up as the Guardian Crane floated downward.

"Emperor warriors," she said.

"Guardian Crane," said Sung and Daniel as they bowed slightly.

"Hey guys!" said Yuka excitedly. "Where's Clara?"

"Hey Yuka," said Daniel as Sung acknowledged her by nodding his chin toward her. "She should be close."

"Did you see the western gate?" asked Sung.

"It's massive!" said Yuka. "And it's beautiful too! So intricate in detail and did you know that the roof is made of…"

"Clawdium," responded Sung and Daniel in unison.

"I guess you heard too," smiled Yuka.

"Hey!" hollered Clara as she walked briskly toward them.

Yuka moved aside and took a few steps toward Clara, "Hey! You made it!"

Clara joined the group and said, "Yep, pulling up the rear as usual. My Guardian Panda told me that the whole roof of the gate is made of…"

"Clawdium," responded everyone with a smile as they shared a laugh.

"Emperor and empress warriors," said the Guardian Tiger. "Welcome to *Seodaemun* of Azen. I believe the one in your world no longer stands. But here on Azen, ours stand as strong as the day it was completed, never to have ever been breached."

"It's really impressive," said Yuka. "Oh, I've already seen most of it, but you should look at it yourself. The first regiment of battle tigers has already secured it."

Sung turned to the Guardian Tiger and entreated, "Oh! Can I visit *Seodaemun?*"

The Guardian Tiger looked at all the fellow guardians as the Guardian Panda sauntered up to join the group. "Yes, you may. It'd be good for you to become familiar with our surroundings. The head of the Prowlers should be on *Seodaemun* itself. He can give you and the other warriors the full tour."

"Awesome!" said Sung enthusiastically.

"Whoa!" exclaimed Yuka as she pointed excitedly. "Whose are those?"

Clara turned her head as a rabbit broke away from a group of rabbits and trudged its way toward the guardians and the warriors. His eyes lit up as Yuka broke from the group with her hands outstretched. The rabbit balked, took a few steps back, and raised a paw in warning. "Stop!" the rabbit said firmly.

Yuka stopped abruptly as the rabbit's voice held her at bay.

"I will not be picked up," said the rabbit firmly.

Clara laughed as she turned to Yuka's disappointed face. "I picked him up the first time I saw him too because he was so cute!"

"You did?" asked Yuka with a grin.

"Warriors, please meet the Panda Kingdom's top medicinist and herbalist, Juju. The rabbit kingdom is responsible for our health," said the Guardian Panda.

Juju approached the group cautiously, and once he felt confident that he wasn't going to be picked up, he introduced himself. "Good evening, empress and emperor warriors. I am Juju, and I will be providing you an antidote to ward off the venom from the *nue's* snake tail should you get bitten during battle."

Juju gingerly pulled around a pouch from his backside, reached in, and pulled out four glass vials. He gave one to each warrior.

"At dinner tonight," Juju continued. "Please swallow its entire contents. One dose will protect you through the course of battle. Is that understood?"

The warriors nodded as Clara held the glass vial between her thumb and index finger in front of her eyes. It was clear, and she couldn't believe that she was about to drink an antidote for the venom from a snake tail on a creature called the *nue*.

"Remember, the antidote will protect you, but should you get bitten, it will be extremely painful," said Juju ominously. "Those wretched snakes are relentless and will sink their long fangs deep into your flesh. If they do, they will bite down so hard that it will be almost impossible to free yourself from their vice-like fangs. So better to avoid getting bit altogether. Is that clear?"

With stunned and blank faces, the warriors nodded slowly.

"Guardians," said Juju. "Here are four vials for each of you as well."

The Guardian Tiger took all four glass vials into his paws and nodded toward Juju. "Thank you, Juju. We are always grateful for you and your kingdom for your help. Where is Eun-ji?"

"Oh, she is already distributing the antidotes to the white tigers as we speak. She didn't want to wait," said Juju.

"Who is Eun-ji?" asked Sung.

Juju turned toward Sung with his large eyes and answered, "She is the White Tiger Kingdom's head medicinist and herbalist."

"Oh, does every kingdom have one?" asked Yuka?

"Yes," said Juju. "We would not survive against any of the Warlock demons. Just look at our size and glorious fine fur. But we found that we could contribute our medicinal skills to the war effort to each kingdom."

"*Gam-sa-ham-ni-da*," said the Guardian Tiger, thanking Juju in Korean.

"You are welcome. The other rabbit leads and their fluffle will make the rounds soon and distribute the vials to all the soldiers before the end of the night. Very well then, I'll hop to it. Guardians, empress and emperor warriors, fight well and watch those snakes."

Juju turned and gently hopped away.

"He's so adorable!" Yuka exclaimed, trying to control her desire to simply hug him.

"He is," echoed Clara as they chuckled.

"What's a fluffle?" asked Daniel.

"That is a group of rabbits," responded the Guardian Buffalo.

"Oh!" said Daniel. "I never knew."

"Let's take that tour now!" said Sung excitedly as he invoked the bridge Qi element while Daniel thrusted through the air. Sung flew over the tent quarters that were being erected and skimmed along the mountainous side toward the far end of the western gate.

"Hmph," said a disappointed Clara as she looked at Yuka.

"I can take you, Empress Warrior Wu," said the Guardian Crane as she lowered herself.

Clara smiled and raced over, "Oh, thank you! I wish I could fly."

"I'll fly alongside you," said Yuka as Clara nodded, harnessing herself in atop the Guardian Crane. Soon enough, Clara was soaring through the air toward the great western gate of *Seodaemun*.

* * *

Later that night, the warriors were gathered around their dinner table. They had just eaten a hearty meal to give them the strength they needed for battle. The excitement they shared as they discussed their observations of *Seodaemun* soon became subdued as the night wore on. The Warlock's *nue* army would arrive the next morning.

Clara looked about the expressions of her fellow warriors and straightened up.

"Ahem, fellow Azen Warriors," she said with some grandiosity. The other warriors looked at her with attention.

"We are here on the eve of battle and to be honest, I'm a bit scared. Especially of the dreaded snake tails. But I know we have each other's backs, and we will prevail over the Warlock's *nue* army."

Everyone nodded, entertained by Clara's deliberate low warrior's voice. "So, let's take out our anti-snake venom medicine and drink to bravery and courage."

Clara waited as each of her fellow warriors found their vial and uncorked it. They held them up and looked to Clara.

She smiled and said, "So here's to not getting bit by a snake. Bottoms up!"

Each of the warriors brought their vial to their lips and swallowed its contents in one big gulp. Suddenly, everyone's eyes squinted as they pressed their hands onto the table. Sung's face winced while Daniel had one eye open. Yuka gasped, and Clara coughed violently.

"Oh my god! That tasted horrible!" Clara exclaimed as she let out another cough.

"Juju did not tell us that it would taste so awful!" uttered Yuka as she dabbed a napkin to her tongue.

"Oh god, never again!" exclaimed Sung as Daniel added, "I'm with you, bro. That tasted like my swim trunks that I forgot to wash."

"Ewww!" exclaimed Sung. "That's gross!"

The laughter of the warriors sung through the night air.

TWENTY - THREE

There was a stale emptiness in the morning air, the silence broken only by the gentle fluttering of the battle banners. The sun had risen behind them, illuminating the rocky canyon walls before them and the wide swarth of land that laid bare.

Clara exhaled. She was now in her battle armor, which she was quite fond of. It transformed her, and just like it did in the last battle, it made her truly feel like a warrior. She was on the lower level of the middle battle fortress. She turned to her left to look at her Guardian Panda. He was watching the bend in the canyon, watching for the enemy that would soon attack the western gate. She peered past him and saw the lines of panda archers, each standing in silent formation in their bamboo armor with their green bamboo helmets. Their quiet discipline was impressive. To her right was the same sight of panda archers. Running down the middle and entire length of the wall was a seemingly endless supply of green jade-tipped arrows.

She cast her eyes over the wall's edge and saw neatly formed square regiments of panda archers below. Beyond that, she saw another line of neat formations alternating between battle tigers and buffalos. In the center, she could make out Sung and Daniel from behind as they rode atop their guardians. Flanking them were the squadrons of cranes and eagles, ready to take off. She could not see Yuka but knew that she was with her Guardian Crane.

"There." The Guardian Panda's curt utterance broke the silence.

Clara quickly looked outward. In the distance, she saw a lone figure almost glide out of the canyon's bend. Her white robes were flowing and glistening in the sunlight as her voluminous black hair swayed gently in the wind.

"Hey, is that your girlfriend?" asked Daniel jokingly as he felt a stirring of hooves.

Sung came to a start and peered outward, trying to see past the battle banners until he saw the solitary female figure. He squinted, and her silhouette in the distance became clear. A rumbling of anger started to swirl within him as he beamed at Daniel and said, "She's not my girlfriend. But yeah, that's Jisoo, I mean the *gumiho* that tricked me."

Sung regripped the harness atop the Guardian Tiger and clenched hard.

"We'll get her," said Daniel.

"No, she's mine," said Sung as he stared at the *gumiho* in the distance.

"Emperor Warrior Kim," admonished the Guardian Tiger. "You will do no such thing. This battle is more important than any one person's revenge. Is that clear?"

Sung nodded and uttered, "Yes Guardian Tiger. The battle is the goal."

"That is right," responded the Guardian Tiger. "Just like before, once the cranes and archers do their part and the *nue* passes the line of no return, we will charge. You and Emperor Warrior Nguyen will leap off and do what your training has taught you to do."

Sung nodded as he continued to watch the solitary *gumiho* walking toward a rocky stump. As she floated on top of it, Sung asked, "What is she doing?"

"Positioning," said the Guardian Tiger. "She wants to watch as the Warlock's army charge from her commanding position."

With his eyes back on the *gumiho*, Sung watched her curiously as he fingered the Claw Staff along his back to feel its reassuring presence. His eyes refocused on the *gumiho,* and he had an eerie feeling that she was looking right at him.

The *gumiho* stood tall. Her white robes draped gently against her silky skin. The foreboding in the air was palpable as she stared down the neat regiments of tigers and buffalos. Behind them, she surveyed the panda archers. With a glance on each side, she took note of the squadrons of cranes and eagles. But she was impressed by the western gate with its formidable stone wall. Along the top, she could see an entire line of panda archers. The large arched gate was open, and she could see the massive Clawdium doors. She must get her *nue* army through, she thought.

Her seductive icy blue eyes scanned the ranks of the tigers until they settled on a human figure atop a white tiger. She smiled as she found the White Tiger Warrior, despite wanting to kill him in their last encounter. But she rather enjoyed siphoning off his Qi in that sensual kiss, and perhaps his rejuvenated self may provide her a second delicious opportunity. She was fond of kissing her victims even though she'd knew she would be killing them, ever so slowly. But that was the price the emperor warriors paid for her sinister pleasure. It was not often that she had the opportunity to siphon off a warrior's Qi through kissing, but when she did, she enjoyed it immensely.

Perhaps that was her mistake that night. She found the young warrior attractive. She'd admired his strong, young athletic body as she siphoned off his Qi. She admitted to herself that she was touched that he was trying to protect her. Foolish of him, but sweet nonetheless. She would have indulged in all his Qi that very first night, but it had taken all her strength to materialize in Azen through one of its mystical pools. By random luck, she appeared through the Origins Pool instead of some far-off isolated pool in Azen, which would end up in a futile trip. Traversing the mystical waters that connected the pools between Azen and Nadi had always been a hazard: Each time she did, it sapped her strength, leaving her in a weakened state. That night when she found the White Tiger Warrior, she wasn't sure if she could cast him under her seductive spell as her strength was still being restored. But on the second night, she could have siphoned off all his Qi in a single kiss. Instead, she enjoyed him, thinking she was safe in the cave, kissing him throughout the night, siphoning off his Qi, one deep kiss at a time. It was more delicious and pleasurable that way. But her plan was upended when she was discovered by the other warriors and guardians.

She smiled as she put aside the momentary revelry of that night. With that thought, her nine white furry tails unfurled from behind her. That day, the warriors would feel the full wrath of Jisoo, the *gumiho*.

Her right arm extended rightward as her upturned palm beckoned the forces beyond the bend. They were waiting silently, their muscular tiger-like bodies pulsated in anticipation. Their claws were fully extended while their ferocious monkey faces were red with unbridled rage. Their snake-like tails slowly twirled in the wind. At her signal, they rushed forward. There were throngs of them, and they filled the canyon beyond the bend.

There were no neat regiments or lines, just a horde of rage and fury embodied in thousands of agile bodies that were ready to tear their enemies asunder. The first line of the *nue* came forth and formed in front of the *gumiho*.

The *gumiho* looked down at them from her rocky perch, then shifted her eyes down the canyon's bend, admiring the endless mass of restless fur. They were bloodthirsty, and she was going to delight in sending them down toward the western gate to satisfy their blood lust.

She looked up directly at her enemies as her pink tongue slowly slid over her red lips. With that, she uttered, "Bring me back the two boy warriors, alive."

Several of the *nues* looked up, the whites of their eyes crisscrossed by pulsating red blood vessels. They nodded in acknowledgment as they stared down at the kingdom soldiers.

"Begin," the *gumiho* said calmly as she tucked her hands into the sleeves of her robe.

They launched their bodies forward, digging their powerful claws into the terrain. Soon, hundreds upon hundreds of *nue* stampeded toward the western gate with an unsatiable desire to tear into flesh.

TWENTY - FOUR

"Here they come!" Sung hollered as he leaned forward, regripped his hold on the harness, and unslung the Claw Staff.

"Steady," said the Guardian Tiger as Daniel, atop the Guardian Buffalo, unsheathed the club horn from his back.

There was movement from the flanks of the tiger and buffalo formations as hundreds of cranes and eagles took to the sky. The cranes' katana wings glinted in the sunlight and as before, their talons gripped leather bundles loaded with weighted jade-tipped darts. The aerial liftoff, with so many cranes and eagles lifting off at once, was so massive it cast a large rolling shadow over the battlefield. The winged elements soon organized into several V-shaped formations.

"Are you ready, Empress Warrior Satoh?" asked the Guardian Crane.

Yuka checked the harness around her waist and tugged gently on the quick release clasp. Her fingertips glided along the Moon Star and around each side of her waist as five replicated moon stars appeared. With a firm nod, she said, "Ready."

"Then, let's dive!" said the Guardian Crane, who took the lead as she squawked to her fellow crane and eagle squadrons.

The winged squadrons dove elegantly, picking up speed as they neared the first rush of *nues*. The *nues* ignored them as they continued to rush down the battlefield, the rumbling of thousands of clawed paws shaking the earth beneath them. A shriek pierced the air as hundreds of leather bundles were unfurled, releasing thousands of weighted jade-tipped darts down toward the *nues*.

The jade tips pointed down as the feathers on the opposite end allowed them to fly straight and true. Hundreds of darts found their marks as squeals of pain erupted from the roaring masses. Many of the *nues* tumbled over each other as other *nues* simply leapt over them. The ones who fell under were soon trampled upon by the steady procession of their kin.

As the winged squadrons flew back, the Guardian Crane looked back and saw that the *nue* frontline was momentarily broken. But new waves of *nues* soon filled in the gaps. The cranes swooped upward and headed back to the western gate.

"It's the panda archers' turn now," said the Guardian Crane.

Yuka turned around toward the *gumiho* and saw a continuous flow of *nues* rounding the bend in the canyon. *There were so many*, she thought.

"Archers!" Xi Peng, the Head of the Pandemonium Squad bellowed out from atop the wall of *Seodaemun*.

Below, the panda leaders of each of the six archer regiments raised a green flag and waved it into the air. The cloth of the green flag ruffled through the air as six-hundred archers pulled back on their long bows, outfitted with heavier arrows with glowing green jade tips. In a swift motion, the panda leaders snapped their green flags downward as they yelled out in Mandarin for *release*, "*Fang jian!*"

Hundreds of arrows sailed through the air, their jade tips shimmering. When they reached their apex, they turned downward. The *nues* didn't break formation until hundreds of arrows found their marks and sank into the *nues'* flesh, causing them to roll over violently. But the waves of rage-filled *nues* behind them trampled over them and continued their stampede forward. They were almost at the halfway point when another volley of arrows rained down on them, taking out hundreds of *nues*. The frontline was forced to scatter as they continued their race toward the western gate.

"There are so many!" said Clara.

"There are," said the Guardian Panda in a worried tone.

"Can't I just create a sinkhole like I did with the demon dogs?" asked Clara.

"This terrain isn't like Jagged Pass. It's mountainous, covered with a layer of dirt. Your sinkhole would not be deep enough, I'm afraid. You can build upwards, but hollowing out dirt would be challenging."

Clara nodded as the panda archers released a third volley of arrows. Suddenly, they started to flow back through the archway in an orderly fashion.

Clara looked upward as the cranes flew back into the sky in formation with another load of jade-tipped darts, hoping to thin out the ranks of the *nues* as much as possible before they reached the tigers and the buffalos.

"I feel useless just standing here," said a frustrated Clara as she looked up toward her Guardian Panda.

"The fight will come to you soon enough, Empress Warrior Wu. The battle for the wall is where you will be fighting," said the Guardian Panda guardedly.

The Guardian Panda peered out and seeing the *nues* were almost near the halfway mark, he nodded to the archers on his left and then to his right atop the wall. The panda leaders of the archers on the wall raised their green flags, and the pandas pulled back on their bows, their jade-tipped arrows at the ready. The green flags snapped downward as the panda leaders yelled in Mandarin for release once more, "*Fang jian!*"

A volley of arrows sailed through the air, and the panda archers let loose two more waves of deadly arrows. The first wave of arrows sunk into their targets but this time, the *nues* from behind did not trample over their fallen *nues*, but scattered around them. The second and third waves of arrows found their marks as hundreds of *nues* were felled by arrows embedded in their backs, heads, or hindlegs. Though fallen, their snake tails still snapped through the air with a life of their own.

As hundreds of snarling *nues* scattered past their fallen peers, others approached the *nues* who were still alive. With their salivating teeth and sharp claws, they snapped away or pulled out the arrows, giving the fallen *nues* a second chance to satisfy their bloodlust.

"We need to slow down the rear ranks," said the Guardian Crane as she flew back toward the bend in the canyon.

"How about a tornado?" asked Yuka confidently as she squinted against the wind rushing into her face.

"Empress Warrior Satoh, I couldn't agree more," said the Guardian Crane as she flew over the masses as four battle cranes flew in a V formation behind her. "Now."

Yuka invoked the tornado Qi element by screaming *tornado* in Japanese, "*tatsumaki!*" As the bluish Qi element danced at her fingertips, she sent it into the center of the *nue* mass, and a tornado erupted in their midst, causing chaos.

Tens of *nues* were swept up into the tornado funnel and despite their roars, they were defenseless in its vortex. It stood in place, but the oncoming *nues* just flowed around it.

Yuka invoked two more devastating tornadoes. But while they slowed the rear ranks of the *nues*, they simply continued to flow forth from the canyon. "There are so many! More than the demon dogs!" Yuka yelled, looking worried.

"Your tornados will only last so long before they dissipate. Throw up a series of air walls, Empress Warrior Satoh, to at least confuse them," said the Guardian Crane.

Yuka nodded as the Guardian Crane swung around, allowing her to invoke several air walls on the terrain. The *nues* barreled into them as other *nues* crashed into them from behind. But they simply climbed over their fallen kin until they passed over the air walls and continued their race toward the western gate. The first tornado dissipated, dropping tens of disoriented *nues* onto the ground. Survivors of the fall wobbled in a daze before shaking it off and continuing the race downward.

Yuka was disappointed that her Qi elemental powers were only temporary, but she invoked another tornado to disrupt the *nues* as the Guardian Crane flew back toward the western gate.

"Ready!" the Guardian Tiger roared.

Hundreds of tigers tensed up and raised their haunches as Sung leaned forward.

"Buffalos, *sừng*!" hollered the Guardian Buffalo for *horns* in Vietnamese as Daniel gritted his teeth and watched in anticipation.

Hundreds of buffalo hooves dug into the earth as their powerful hind legs prepared to push forward. The buffalos soon lowered their heads and closed their eyes as the muscles around the base of their horns pulsated as the massive horns rotated forward before locking into place.

"So awesome," said Daniel as he looked down at the Guardian Buffalo's horns that pointed toward the *nues*.

As the first *nue* crossed the midway point of the battlefield, both the Guardian Tiger and Buffalo ordered in unison to *attack* and *charge* in Korean and Vietnamese, "*Gong gyuck! Thủ lao!*"

The ground beneath them shook as hundreds of thick paws and heavy hooves pounded the ground, raising dirt into the air.

The battle tigers and buffalos raced forward to meet their enemy. The *nues'* menacing and contorted monkey faces came into clear view.

Sung rose onto his knees atop the Guardian Tiger. In an instant before the clash of powerful claws ripping through the air, he leapt upwards, invoked the bridge Qi element, and sailed atop its tip. But as he re-oriented himself in the air, the ice beneath him crumbled away, and he suddenly found himself falling with his arms flailing. Before he could think of what to do next, his hand was grabbed by Daniel, who was soaring above him.

"They literally clawed your ice sculpture to pieces!" teased Daniel. "Fire!"

"And ice!" screamed Sung with a grin as he invoked another ice bridge with a much-bigger base. When the tip reached Sung's feet, Daniel let him go, and Sung quickly surveyed the carnage below. He saw that the Guardian Tiger was slashing his way through the *nues* while the Guardian Buffalo was goring the *nues* who dared to get close to him. It was a gruesome and bloody scene of flesh and fur being torn away from the *nues*, whose blood splattered into the air.

Daniel sent down fireball after fireball, setting *nues* ablaze, but their mindless rage only propelled their flame-engulfed bodies toward the western gate before they collapsed.

As Sung invoked his deadly icicles, he had to ground his footing as the *nues* clawed mercilessly at the base of his ice bridge, shaking it. *These nues were strong—stronger than the demon dogs*, he thought. He glanced to his side and saw his Guardian Tiger along with the Prowlers, clawing ferociously at the *nues*. Their meshed bodysuit armor was holding up. The Guardian Buffalo was holding his own along with the Rammers, who were ramming mercilessly into their enemies as the sound of cracking bones filled the air.

Sung looked beyond the chaos of what seemed to be a thousand battle tigers and buffalos engaged in the most horrific battle he had ever witnessed. The few *nues* that did get past the battle scrimmage were shot down with arrows from the western gate. For a moment, he marveled at the western gate, with its two-tiered battle fortress clad in an impregnable Clawdium roof. He thought back for a moment and realized how the western gate was no longer standing back in Korea, and here it was, on Azen, in a much more majestic form. His mind suddenly went to this father and he wished he could see him defending a vestige of Korean pride. He welled up in emotion and let out a nostalgic battle cry, "*Seodaemun!*"

Sung turned toward the *gumiho* with determination and despite the hordes of *nues* still racing past, he saw her. Her hair flowing from the rush of *nues* passing by. She calmly watched the calamitous fighting before her with not a care in the world. This angered him.

"Hey!" said Yuka as she soared toward him and hovered in front of him, throwing down a flurry of moon stars that sank into the snake heads. "Are you just going to stare at her from your icy pedestal or fight?"

"Right," said Sung. "There are so many!"

"That's what I keep on saying! My tornadoes aren't killing them all, and they can only suck up those who are close by," lamented Yuka as two of her tornadoes dissipated, releasing their dizzy victims. She quickly invoked two more toward the back.

Soon, Daniel joined them. "I'm sending down fireballs, but there's no end in sight to these *nues!*"

"We just need to slow them down," said Yuka. "Let's throw up as many walls toward the back so that the tigers and buffalos are not outnumbered."

"Sounds like a plan!" said Sung, and with Yuka on his right and Daniel to his left, they started to invoke ice, air, and fire walls to block the oncoming *nues*. The appearance of ice and fire walls paused the *nues*, but they simply flowed around the walls. The invisible walls caused mass confusion as the *nues* snapped into the air and struggled to find their way around them.

Delaying the *nues* gave the tigers and buffalos the much-needed space to do their job, but they were tiring. Battle fatigue was setting in as the tigers and buffalos panted, their endurance taxed beyond their capacity.

The Guardian Tiger was locked claw-to-claw with a *nue*, whose snake-like tail was snapping at him. But he held his ground and dug in his hind legs. The Guardian Tiger was equally matched with the *nue*, but found he had to bob his head as the snake tail tried to sink its venomous fangs into him. In one last effort, the Guardian Tiger roared into the face of the *nue*, whose monkey-like head suddenly drooped as Sung's Claw Staff slammed into it. The *nue* dropped to the ground as Sung stepped up to the Guardian Tiger and asked, "Are you okay?"

The Guardian Tiger grinned and said *thank you* in Korean, "Yes, *gam-sa-ham-ni-da*, Emperor Warrior Kim. We still have more fighting to do."

Sung nodded and spun around with his staff. He steeled himself on the battle ground as the Guardian Tiger settled onto all fours beside him and roared at the oncoming *nues*. The Guardian Tiger lunged ahead, clawing at the closest *nue* while another *nue* leapt straight for Sung.

He sidestepped the *nue* and when it landed, slammed the tip of his staff on top of the *nue's* head before it could react. As Sung spun around, he could only catch the fangs of the *nue* coming at him as he instinctively braced his staff in front of him. The *nue's* mouth gripped the staff, and Sung clenched his fists around the staff as he fell back, hitting the ground with a thud. But he stayed focused on the *nue*, who was trying to rip his staff away or bite through it. Suddenly, he saw the *nue's* eyes focus on the blue jade. In an instant, the *nue's* teeth snapped closer to the blue jade as Sung struggled to keep it away. Hot saliva from the *nue* dripped onto his face. He was disgusted but his eyes lit up at the sight of the snake tail. Knowing he was immune from its venom, he was only worried about the dreaded bite.

But as the *snake tail* reared its head to strike, an arrow buried itself in its mouth, and the force ripped the entire snake tail from the *nue's* backside. The *nue* suddenly looked up as another arrow sunk into its forehead. Its entire body fell limp. Sung pushed himself out from under the dead *nue* and hastily got up as he spotted Clara.

"I couldn't just stand there at the gate while you guys were fighting," Clara shouted as she quickly released two more arrows, which whizzed by Sung and sunk into the foreheads of two more *nues*.

"I can't blame you!" yelled a grateful Sung as he quickly slammed his staff against an oncoming *nue*. "Let's go up and see what's happening!"

Clara nodded and invoked the pillar Qi element and rose atop of it as Sung spiraled around it with an ice bridge. Soon Yuka and Daniel, exasperated, flew to them and hovered nearby while they surveyed the battlefront.

"It looks like the last wave made it around the bend," said Yuka.

"It still looks like hundreds," said Daniel.

The worried warriors looked down to where the tigers and buffalos were still engaged in a brutal fight. But now they were being assisted by the cranes, who were able to dart in with their katana wings to slice apart the *nues*.

"They're exhausted," said Sung. "We need to take the final part of this fight to *Seodaemun!*"

Everyone nodded as Sung asked Clara, "Can you create a wall from one end of the canyon to the other? You can create the longest structures out of all of us."

"I can try," said Clara. She bit her lip as she scanned the width of the canyon floor. It had to be about five hundred feet. She invoked the *wall* Qi element as she hollered out in Cantonese, "*Ten-bing!*" She pointed at one end of the canyon as the dirt wall began to erupt from the ground. Then she whisked her finger to the other end to complete a ten-foot-high wall. "Yes!" she exclaimed under her breath.

The Guardian Crane swooped in and said, "Back to the wall!"

The remaining tigers and buffalos dispatched the last of the *nues* left on the wrong side of the dirt wall and started their retreat. The littered bodies of *nues* were everywhere, along with a few fallen tigers and buffalos. Large eagles swooped in and with their hefty talons, carried away the injured tigers and buffalos.

"You two go ahead!" said Daniel. "Yuka and I will give them one last surprise."

Clara stood atop her dirt column and looked back toward the western gate when Sung came up alongside her on a new ice bridge.

"Care for a lift?" he asked.

Clara smiled, caught off guard. "Sure."

"Step here," Sung said as he pointed in front of his feet.

Clara carefully stepped onto the ice bridge and found her footing. She flinched a bit as Sung's left arm slid smoothly around her waist, causing her to look up at him. He tightened his grasp around her waist and said, "Hold on tight!"

He invoked an ice bridge, and they surfed on its tip toward the western gate. As she clutched the Bow of Destiny to her chest, she instinctively reached over with her right hand and grabbed Sung's hand, still on her waist. He didn't lose any focus as he forged the ice bridge forward until finally, they reached the wall's edge.

"Your stop," he said jovially.

Clara looked up and nodded as she stepped off the tip of the ice bridge. With a helping paw from the Guardian Panda, she hopped onto the wall. Sung did the same, then turned and invoked the evaporate Qi element as the ice bridge dissipated.

Clara scanned the battlefield. The *nues* were clawing through several areas of the dirt wall, and some were simply climbing over the earthen wall. However, the dirt wall did its job in slowing down the remaining *nues*. Suddenly two tornadoes infused with fire spiraled upward. They sucked up the nearby *nues* and burned them alive in their fiery vortexes. The tornadoes were causing mayhem behind the earthen wall. She could see Daniel and Yuka flying back in a hurry.

A loud sound of heaving metal reverberated through the air. Clara peered over and saw the two massive Clawdium doors moving inward, each door pulled by a massive chain through the tunnel. Clara backed away a few steps and turned. She ran to the other side of the wall and could see ten large buffalos pulling on the other ends of the metal chain to pull the outer doors shut. When the outer doors came together, she heard a loud clanking noise reverberate through the tunnel below. Curious, she descended the stairs and out of the wall. She turned her gaze down the arched tunnel before her. Sung soon made his way down, and Yuka and Daniel also floated down to witness the sealing of the great western gate of *Seodaemun*. Soon the detached chains were pulled away, and they could see a large metal rod being inserted into the large metal loops of the outer Clawdium doors from the inside. Then two more solid Clawdium barriers slid into place from within the tunnel's side. Finally, the inner Clawdium doors were pushed into place by the same buffalos. As the two doors met, a low but solid thud echoed through the air as two large metal rods slid into place.

The warriors could see why *Seodaemun* was never breached. They prepared for the final onslaught.

TWENTY - FIVE

"They're almost through!" exclaimed Clara anxiously as she peered out into the battlefield.

The base of the earthen wall that she had invoked earlier was crumbling as the *nues* clawed at it relentlessly from the other side. The few that managed to climb over were quickly met with deadly arrows.

Yuka's chest plate heaved as she took in measured breaths. Her battle armor gave her stature, keeping her back and shoulders straight. Her battle helmet gave her face a warrior's look of power. The red flare that swooped back along the top of her helmet gave her pride. With her feet a shoulder's width apart and her hands lightly pressing the moon stars along her waist, she looked poised to take on the entire *nue* army herself.

Yuka nodded, and Clara quickly glanced past her. Further along the wall stood Daniel. He was determined as well as he looked down at Clara's earthen wall, feeling the wall of *Seodaemun* beneath his fingertips. He knew that it was only a matter of moments before the earthen wall would crumble, letting hundreds of *nues* rush toward them in a wild frenzy.

Clara turned to her left and saw Sung. *How tall he was*, she thought, *and how the battle armor flattered his athletic frame.* The way he faced the imminent fall of the wall with such resolve reminded Clara of some of the dutiful Korean soldiers of ancient Korea depicted in the K-dramas she had seen. Suddenly he turned to her, and their eyes met. Clara couldn't help staring, and he nodded. Clara smiled and felt a moment of embarrassment as she turned her attention back to the battlefield.

As if on cue, rumbling could be heard from the center of the earthen wall as it started to fall. The noise reverberated along the wall until a crescendo of tumbling earth was heard. An immense cloud of dust erupted into the air, obscuring the battlefield as a seemingly endless torrent of *nues* rushed forth.

"*Fang jian!*" as the Guardian Panda said in Mandarin to *release* as hundreds of panda archers released their arrows. The plucks of the bow strings sang through the air, and though the arrows were accurate, it would take more than hundreds of arrows to slow down this last torrent of *nues*.

Clara reached back and pulled out her last arrow, cocked it, and released it as it sunk itself into the hind leg of a *nue*, only slowing it down. Before Clara could even turn to replenish her arrows, a panda attendant shoved a new bundle of arrows into her quiver. Clara nodded, but her gesture went unnoticed as several panda attendants were doing the same across the entire line of panda archers.

"They're at the wall!" screamed Yuka as she threw several of her moon stars toward the *nues*, lodging them into their eyes or the snapping snake tails.

Clara went through another quiver full of arrows and without even turning, a new bundle of arrows had been loaded into her quiver, and she continued on. Both Sung and Daniel were throwing icicles and fireballs at the *nues*.

As solid as *Seodaemun* was, Clara felt the jolt of hundreds of *nues* slamming into the stone wall of the western gate. They were massing at the base, climbing on top of each other and slowly piling up. Blood seeped from the arrows that dug into their flesh, but they held steadfast, and their muscular agility gave them the fortitude to withstand the pain.

Clara peered over the wall, where four towers of entwined *nue* bodies were slowly making their way up the wall. Arrows were zinging through the air as the pandas furiously fired arrows at the *nue* masses. Roars of agony made Clara look right as she saw the base of the pile of *nues* crumble and several *nues* burst into flames. But as their bodies fell, other *nues* callously pulled the injured *nues* aside and rushed back up. Their bloodlust was insatiable.

"There's still so many!" Yuka yelled out as the *nues* were halfway up the wall.

Clara turned around as she heard the thunderous noise of hundreds of tigers ascend the stone stairs and line up along the wall behind her. The Guardian Tiger walked up to Sung, who was still slinging icicles at the mass of *nues* closest to him. The Guardian Tiger looked out, and though the *gumiho* had sent in her last wave of *nues*, the last wave was her most resilient, enhanced with a tougher furry hide.

The Guardian Tiger marched over to where the Guardian Panda and Clara were. The Guardian Panda released an arrow and looked up at his old friend.

"How are we doing?" asked the Guardian Tiger.

"Their fur is tougher with this wave. Even our arrows are having a hard time, but they will fall," said the Guardian Panda.

"If they crest the wall's edge, fall back and we'll fight them, claw-to-claw," said the Guardian Tiger gravely. "We must hold this wall."

"You can't!" Clara screamed. "There's too many."

"We've done this before, we are ready for the sacrifice," said the Guardian Tiger.

Hopelessness filled Clara's heart as she saw that the mesh bodysuit armor of the Guardian Tiger was now slit and torn in several places, exposing him to more painful slashes. She didn't want any more pain to come to the battle soldiers of Azen.

Clara's eyes lit up as she spun around toward Yuka and whispered into her ear. Yuka nodded and ran toward Daniel.

"Just continue to hold them off!" said Clara. "I have a plan."

Clara ran to Sung and grabbed him by his right bicep when he was just about to invoke another icicle. He gave her a startled look as she said to him, "Pillars and ice!"

Sung's expression was clear and despite his tired arm, he walked to the edge of the wall with Clara.

She leaned precariously over the wall and met Yuka's gaze from the other end. She gave Clara a nod. She pulled back and invoked a tornado about a hundred feet out and Daniel fed it with a stream of fire. The *nues* who were too close were sucked in immediately, which forced the remaining *nues* to race toward the wall.

Yuka created three additional tornados as Daniel fed them a stream of fire. The churning tornados created winds that lashed at the walls, forcing some of the panda archers to pull back.

"Pillars!" said Sung. "We need to hurry!"

Clara nodded and she braced herself against the force of the tornado's wind. She invoked a pair of earthen pillars on each side of the first mass of *nues*, who were scrambling toward the top of the wall. The pillars rose several stories into the air, and she looked at Sung.

Sung shot his hand upward and invoked a thick ice bridge spanning the two earthen pillars. All eyes shot up to witness the huge slab of ice precariously spanning the two wobbling earthen pillars.

"Now!" said Sung as he stepped back.

Clara quickly invoked the flatten Qi element, and the earthen pillars collapsed, sending the ice slab crashing down onto the *nues*. As the slab of ice skimmed the wall, it scraped the *nues* off, crushing them below.

Without a word, Clara invoked another set of pillars targeting the mass of *nues* farthest away on her left, which Sung spanned with another massive slab of ice. Clara leaned to her right and invoked another two pairs of earthen pillars. When Sung started to invoke his ice bridge, he said to Clara with conviction, "Crush 'em!"

Clara readily invoked the flatten Qi element, sending the large slab of ice tumbling onto the mass of frantic *nues* as their bodies buckled under the weight of the ice. Clara did the same for the last two pairs of earthen pillars, and the slabs of ice crashed onto the *nues* without mercy.

Yuka invoked the evacuate Qi element, and the tornados simply vanished as the blackened bodies of *nue* fell to the ground in a dead heap of muscle and bones.

The remaining *nues* scattered, their roars disjointed. Some continued to claw hopelessly at the wall, others ran randomly about, and still others ran away from the wall.

"Archers!" hollered the Guardian Panda as all the pandas stepped forward and cocked their bows. "Let none escape."

The panda archers released an onslaught of arrows until a final squeal of death was heard and silence fell onto the bloodied battlefield.

Clara exhaled and felt a burden fall away. She no longer feared for the safety of her fellow warriors, but more importantly, she felt she spared the battle tigers unnecessary death.

"Well done," said the Guardian Panda.

"It was all of us," responded Clara.

Sung came up to her with excitement in his eyes as he raised his palm toward her. Clara happily slapped it back and let out a much-needed giggle.

"We were awesome!" exclaimed Sung as he raised his palm toward the Guardian Panda, who stared back at him with his brown eyes. Sung awkwardly shifted in his feet and he was left hanging and said, "Uh, you slap my hand, it's called a high five."

The Guardian Panda looked at his much bigger palm and slapped Sung's palm hard, causing Sung to wince in silent pain. Clara chuckled as the Guardian Tiger sauntered over, "Very impressive, you two."

"Thank you," said Clara and Sung.

"The cranes will fly out and assess the battlefield before we reopen the gate to clear it. But today, *Seodaemun*, has held once more," the Guardian Tiger said proudly.

"*Seodaemun!*" screamed Sung with Korean pride.

Then from afar, someone screamed out "*Seodaemun!*"

Both Clara and Sung looked down the wall and saw Yuka and Daniel waving and giving a thumbs up. Soon, the battle tigers erupted in a victorious battle cry of, "*Seodaemun!*"

"Hey," said Sung curiously as his eyes shifted to the far end of the battlefield. "She's still there!"

"Who?" asked Clara as she followed him to the edge of the wall.

"Jisoo," he said scornfully.

Clara looked out and she could see the faint outline of the *gumiho* and her flaring furry tails waving gently in the air.

Clara pulled out an arrow and loaded it into the Bow of Destiny. She squinted her eye and released it.

Though the *gumiho* was over a thousand feet away, Clara's jade-tipped arrow flew straight and true. The *gumiho* came clearer into view and didn't look the slightest bit fazed. The green jade arrow tip glinted in the air just as the icy blue eyes of the *gumiho* glistened. The arrow passed harmlessly through her body as it dissipated, and she was gone.

TWENTY - SIX

The stars were bright that early evening. Some brighter than others. The four warriors, still in their loosened battle armor, cast their eyes upward.

"It's insane that we're on another world," said Sung.

"Uh-huh," said Clara.

"It reminds me of the stars back at camp," said Yuka.

"I can't believe we're here just looking up at the stars when a few hours ago, we were fighting hundreds of monsters," said Daniel.

"That's what warriors do," said Sung with a hint of smugness.

"Sorry we couldn't get your girlfriend," teased Daniel.

"Hey!" said Sung teasingly. "She's not my girlfriend. Besides, Clara tried to take her out."

"And?" asked Daniel.

"Poof!" said Clara as she gestured with her hands. "She was gone in a white puff of smoke."

"Do you really think her name is Jisoo?" asked Daniel.

"Who knows and who cares," said Sung disdainfully. "All I know is she didn't win today."

Everyone nodded in agreement as Clara looked down at her boots.

"Emperor and empress warriors," said the Guardian Tiger as the other guardians followed him.

The warriors stood up, picked up their helmets and weapons, and faced their guardians.

The Guardian Tiger was still in his meshed bodysuit armor, which bore the tears of battle. But his white-and-black striped fur was still bold, and his steely blue eyes pierced the early evening shadows.

"Warriors, the kingdoms, but especially the White Tiger Kingdom, thank you for your efforts today. Because of you, we ended up with only minor causalities and minimal losses. But more importantly, *Seodaemun* was not breached!"

Sung nodded with pride as he looked at Clara.

"We're clearing the battlefield, but for now, you will be flying back to your kingdoms for a full meal before you depart for your home tomorrow," said the Guardian Tiger.

"Once you are ready, please find the cranes down the path, and we'll leave," said the Guardian Tiger. He bowed along with the rest of the guardians who turned toward the awaiting cranes.

"Wow, another battle done," said Clara.

"Yah, just two more," said Sung wistfully.

"I just want to lie down in my bed at Crane Castle and sleep," said Yuka.

"Man, we need to visit each other's kingdoms!" said Sung.

"Yah, let's make sure we do that," said Daniel wishfully. "I'm sure the guardians won't mind when we return the next time."

Everyone nodded, knowing that they would be parting ways once more. Clara looked up at everyone and brought her clenched fists to her chest with her elbows out. Sung, Yuka, and Daniel smiled and did the same. As they nodded to each other, they uttered, "For Azen."

The warriors walked down the path and saw the Guardian Panda, Buffalo, and Tiger, each straddling an eagle this time. The Guardian Crane was talking with three other cranes when she saw the approaching warriors.

"*Konbanwa*," said Yuka to the Guardian Crane in Japanese for *good evening*.

"*Konbanwa*, Empress Warrior Satoh," the Guardian Crane responded. "Are we ready to go?"

"Mmmm… yes, we are," said Yuka.

Each of the warriors bowed and went to their designated crane. They greeted their cranes and gently climbed aboard them. Once harnessed in, they patted the nape of their crane's neck as the crane nodded.

With lofty grace, the Guardian Crane bearing Yuka flew upward followed by the others. Once in formation, the warriors and guardians flew into the tranquil night as the moons and stars shimmered in the night sky.

TWENTY - SEVEN

Clara's hands pressed against her folded training top as she placed it onto a neat pile of Azen clothing in her room at Bamboo Tower. Her eyes rested for a moment on the two bamboo warrior medallions, the small illumination jade souvenir, and the Azen jade bracelet that were on the tabletop. Her eyes shifted to the low table where the Bow of Destiny rested in its rack with her quiver lying beneath it. Her light gray-green jade-dusted battle armor hung in its battle wardrobe in magnificence. How she wished she could take the armor back home! She could wear it for Halloween, and none would be the wiser, she thought. Only she would know that she was the Empress Warrior of the Panda Kingdom of Azen. She chuckled at the thought of having to explain this to her parents and how cosplay was her new hobby.

A knock came on the door, and she stood up as the Guardian Panda entered. Clara bowed slightly and was caught off guard when the Panderess also entered the room, wearing a red top with golden embroidery. Her face was calming and bore a smile. Her bow was deeply respectful, and Clara bowed in kind.

"*Ni hao*, Empress Warrior Wu," greeted the Panderess with *hello* in Mandarin.

"*Ni hao*, Panderess," Clara said respectfully.

"I heard you fought well yesterday," she said gratefully. "For that, on behalf of the Panda Kingdom, thank you for your service."

"You are welcome," responded Clara as she blushed at the praise. "We all fought well."

"Yes indeed. Well, Guardian Panda will fly out with you to the Portal Circle, where a wonderful lunch has been prepared for you and the other warriors before you return to your home world. Until then, please take good care of yourself."

"I will, Panderess," said Clara as she bowed slightly to her, who bowed again and exited.

"Are you ready to go, Empress Warrior Wu?" asked the Guardian Panda. "The cranes are ready to fly us back to the Portal Circle."

"Gotcha," said Clara wistfully. "I'll be out in a second."

The Guardian Panda nodded and exited Clara's room, leaving the door open as he waited outside.

Clara checked her t-shirt and brushed down her buttoned-down sweater and jeans. She looked down at her socks and wiggled her toes. She was about to bound for her shoes when she paused. She walked back to the bamboo table and picked up the two warrior medallions, Hong in her left hand and Hua Mulan in the other. The wise words of the emperor warrior of the Panda Kingdom who had retrieved the first Bamboo Jade stayed with her: "Remain true." Her eyes turned to the medallion for Hua Mulan and smiled. "We're related, I know it." She then tucked both into her back pocket and bounded for the door, where she paused to slip into her shoes.

"Ready!" Clara said jovially as the Guardian Panda's eyes blinked at her.

They took the lift to the hangar level and greeted the two cranes. Shiori greeted Clara, and she happily nodded back at her. She climbed aboard, harnessed herself in, and soon, she flew out with her Guardian Panda toward the Portal Circle.

* * *

"Mmmm! They have *tempura*!" Yuka squealed in delight.

"Oh my god, I'm stuffed. I thought the dinner back at Claw Mountain last night was something, but this is just as delicious," Sung raved.

"You're telling me, the food at the palace yesterday was amazing," Daniel added. "But I did feel a little guilty for eating so much."

"I think we should eat as much as possible," said Clara. "After the next two battles, we may never be able to visit Azen ever again."

Everyone nodded wistfully.

"So, it's back to being high school kids again," said Sung.

"Yah, what double lives we live," Clara said reflectively.

"I don't mind it. At least here on Azen, I'm free to be a warrior with powers," said Yuka as she grinned.

"Oh man, I just remembered, I portal'ed here right before dinner. *Eomma* is going to be so angry with me," said Sung.

Everyone laughed, "Oh shoot, me too," said Clara. "Maybe I'll stay for a few more hours and manifest more."

"That's a good idea," said Yuka. "I don't mind staying longer."

"Do we even know what day it is?" asked Daniel.

Everyone looked at each other blankly until they all laughed.

"Bro, you're so right!" said Sung.

"I forgot," said Yuka.

"I arrived a couple of days earlier," said Clara with an uncertain tone. "So, I really don't know."

"The Portal Book will know," said Sung confidently.

Everyone looked at each other with a smirk and nodded in agreement. They moved away from the meal table and began walking toward the Portal Circle. Sung and Daniel walked ahead as they jostled with each other. Yuka came up beside Clara and slid her left hand inside of Clara's right elbow. Clara looked at Yuka with grinning affection and gently placed her left hand on Yuka's as they sauntered up the knoll toward the Portal Circle.

"I like the robes," said Clara as she looked up and down Daniel's frame, which was draped in a red robe as he was in shorts. "The way it seals up magnetically is really cool."

"It is," replied Yuka. "Maybe he'll remember to wear warmer clothes next time. I like Sung's pants, they look very comfortable too."

"Those sweats?" asked Clara rhetorically as she glanced at Sung's navy blue sweats. "Yah, they do. How about you? It looks like a school uniform."

"Oh, this?" Yuka replied questioningly. "Yah, there's a school on the camp with a lot of classes for different things. I have a lot of time for that these days."

"I know what you mean," said Clara grinningly. "But I don't mind

Chinese school now. I have a reason now."

"Me too with Japanese school," said Yuka. "Do you manifest the Qi elements during your spare time?"

"Yep, when I can… oh, the guardians are at the Portal Circle," said Clara causing Yuka to look up.

The warriors walked into the Portal Circle and their guardian animals were at their designated spots.

"Good afternoon," said the Guardian Tiger as the fur around his snout moved with every movement of his mouth. "I hope your lunch was satisfying."

"Most definitely, Guardian Tiger," said Sung.

"Very good," said the Guardian Tiger. "Before you are sent back to your own world, your guardians and I wanted to say how impressed we are with your bravery and courage. Azen, its kingdoms, and the protection of the Portal Books are in your debt."

The warriors looked humbled and grinned awkwardly from the praise.

"Before you go…" said the Guardian Tiger before he paused when he saw Sung raise his hand. "Yes, Emperor Warrior Kim?"

"Would it be possible for us to hang around and manifest? When I left, it was just about dinner time and I just ate so much at lunch, my *eomma* would be mad that I would not be hungry."

The Guardian Tiger's eyebrow rose before it settled back down, "Well, we wouldn't want to make your *eomma* displeased by your lack of appetite."

The Guardian Tiger continued, "Emperor and empress warriors, you are more than welcome to stay for however long you want this afternoon. During this time, your guardians and I will attempt to help you manifest new Qi elements with you. Also, we want you to know, that you can also think of new Qi elements once you are at home. Yes, Empress Warrior Wu?"

"What do you mean, we can think of new Qi elements?" asked Clara as she put her hand down.

"For example, you were not successful in manifesting mud, but you can continue to try. But if you can think of other words to control the earth beneath you, you may be able to manifest it while you are home. We won't know how successful it would be until you return to Azen, but you are free to explore your capabilities with the Portal Books in your world."

There was collective surprise from the warriors as Clara echoed everyone's thoughts, "Whoa, I didn't know that. We can try to master new Qi elements back in our world?"

"Yes," said the Guardian Tiger.

"Like, I can manifest a snowball?" asked Sung?

"Yes, a snowball is a known Qi element, but it serves very little use in battle," said the Guardian Tiger.

"Yes, Guardian Tiger," said Sung respectfully. "I think I understand: battle-worthy Qi elements only."

"Very well then," said the Guardian Tiger. "Please manifest away or relax before your..."

The Guardian Tiger stopped in the middle of his sentence as he saw that all the warriors turned around quickly to manifest more Qi elements in their Portal Books. His mouth closed as he glanced at all the other guardians before he walked over to Sung.

"It's still not manifesting," Clara said begrudgingly as the black Chinese character for mud just stared back at her.

"It's okay," said the Guardian Panda. "Not all warriors invoke the same Qi elements. What else can you make with the earth?"

Clara's eyes looked up into the corner of her brain when they turned toward the Guardian Panda and she said, "How about a dust storm?"

The Guardian Panda smiled and said, "You may try."

Clara brushed out the Chinese character for dust storm and nothing happened. She tried again, but still nothing. But on the third try, the fiery embers swirled from within the black character, floated off the page, and seeped into Clara's chest.

"Yes!" said Clara with a big giddy smile.

The Guardian Panda smiled and remarked, "Continue to manifest."

Clara nodded and continued to manifest more Qi elements along with her fellow warriors over the next couple of hours.

"I think it's time for me to go back," said Daniel as he stepped back from the Portal Book and turned around to face his friends.

"Okay, bro," said Sung. "Have a good trip home."

Daniel glanced at the guardians, bowed, and turned to his Guardian Buffalo, "Guardian Buffalo, thank you for everything. I… I learned a lot about myself this time. *Cảm ơn bạn.*"

The Guardian Buffalo nodded and replied, "Each day should be a learning experience."

Daniel turned and jovially let out, "See everyone soon!"

The warriors waved as Daniel turned, gave his robe to a buffalo attendant, and stepped out of his shoes. He began to brush the Vietnamese word for home into his Portal Book. As the bright white light started to emanate from the book, Daniel gently closed his eyes. The light soon engulfed him, leaving no trace of him once the light had faded.

"Emperor Warrior Kim," said the Guardian Tiger.

"Me? Sure thing," said Sung as he slid out of his shoes. He turned over his shoulder to look at Clara and Yuka and said, "Take care, see you soon!"

Clara and Yuka waved as Sung brushed the Korean word for home into the Portal Book. Like Daniel, he closed his eyes until the bright light engulfed him, whisking him through the Portal Book and back to his home on earth.

"That is so amazing," said Yuka. "Okay, Clara, I will see you soon!"

"Take care of yourself!" said Clara as she waved to Yuka, who said goodbye to her Guardian Crane. And in an instant, she too was gone in a flash of light.

"That now leaves you, Empress Warrior Wu," said the Guardian Panda.

Clara nodded. "Guardian Panda," asked Clara.

"Yes, Empress Warrior Wu," the Guardian Panda responded.

"Why do I feel so comfortable being Chinese here?" asked Clara.

The Guardian Panda looked at Clara curiously and simply said, "Why shouldn't you be comfortable with being Chinese anywhere?"

Clara stared into the Guardian Panda's blank white-and-black expression and smiled, "You're right. I'll see you soon, then."

"Yes, you will, Empress Warrior Wu," the Guardian Panda said as Clara finished brushing out the Chinese character for home.

Clara stared at the character and said it in her mind as the white glow started to radiate out from the book. She looked down and caught the glint of light from the jade bracelet that her mother had given her. Her hand pressed against it before she closed her eyes as the white light engulfed her.

TWENTY - EIGHT

The warm glow of the white light faded away, and Daniel opened his eyes. Soon, the Portal Book on his desk came into view, and he straightened up a bit and looked around his room. Nothing seemed amiss. He jolted up and toward his bed and picked up his phone. The black screen woke up and "5:24 PM" showed on the display. His mother would be home soon. He quickly scanned his somewhat untidy bedroom before spying a pair of jeans on the floor. He slipped out of his shorts, grabbed the jeans, and slid them on in a hurry. He found a pair of socks on the rug and put those on before dashing out of his bedroom and down the flight of stairs. He put on his sneakers, grabbed his keys from the entry table before dashing out the back door.

He exited onto the back porch of his townhouse. All seemed normal in Houston. His eyes darted left and right. None of his neighbors were out. He bolted down the concrete steps and crossed the small backyard. He jumped to grab the top of the wooden fence, pulled himself over, and landed on the other side with a thud. He paused, looking furtively around his neighbor's yard. When he was sure he wasn't bringing any attention to himself, he bolted through the yard and up their driveway until he made his way to the street. From there, he turned right and ran.

As he ran, his heart was steady. He was in the best shape of his life, both from his swimming and his training on Azen. To the few pedestrians he encountered, he was just an athletic teenager on a run. He rounded the corner and ran about fifty feet when he saw his mother up ahead. He knew it was her, from her straight black hair and her gait. As usual, she appeared to be holding a brown shopping bag in her hands. She was just about to turn the corner down their street when Daniel's eyes furrowed at the now-familiar navy-blue car that had just passed him on his left.

The navy-blue car cruised down the street with music playing through its open windows. The man with the shaved head snickered as he pointed out Daniel's mother to the driver, a man with disheveled dirty blonde hair.

"Hey!" the man with the shaved head said. "There's that Asian chick, let's see if I can get her attention this time."

The driver laughed as he brought his car to a stop at the intersection. His friend pointed down the street at the trailing figure of Daniel's mother as he turned to him with a snicker. The driver laughed when suddenly, his eyes bulged at seeing his friend's arm yanked out of the window and his head slammed against the upper door frame as his face winced in pain. Suddenly, a hand reached inside and pulled on the door handle, forcing it open. With his arm still pulled through the window, the man on the passenger side tumbled out and found himself being yanked away by his neck.

With his arm released, the man looked up and saw Daniel beaming down at him. *It was just a kid,* he thought. He barreled upward in anger and shoved Daniel back a few feet.

"What the hell is your problem, kid!" the man yelled as he huffed in anger.

Daniel stood tall with his lightly clenched fists and firmly responded, "I'm just gonna say this once, leave Asian women alone!"

The man's cocky face suddenly broke into a laugh as his friend got out of the driver side of the car. His expression became angry as he lunged at Daniel. "I'll do whatever I…"

Daniel quickly sidestepped him and brought his elbow to the man's face, and his cheeks wobbled from the swift force of the impact. He hobbled backwards as blood flowed from his nostrils. He quickly wiped his nose and was startled at the amount of blood on his hand. He looked up at Daniel and started to charge at him when his chin was met with a swift kick, sending him crashing backwards against the open passenger side door.

Daniel quickly spun around and dodged a wide right hook from the driver, who'd come around the car. His overextended wide punch spun him around to face Daniel. Daniel swiftly landed a powerful side kick to his chest, sending him tumbling into his friend against the passenger side door, which creaked on impact.

As the two men struggled atop each other, they cowered against the car door with their hands raised to ward off their attacker. Daniel stood over them and crouched down, causing them to tremble a bit.

"Wallets," said Daniel.

The two men looked at each other bewildered until Daniel said firmly once more, "Wallets!"

"You want our money kid?" said the driver as he reached into his back pocket and pulled out his wallet. "Here, take it."

Daniel snatched it and beamed at the other man as he struggled with his wallet before flicking it toward Daniel. With both wallets in hand, Daniel gave them a firm look. He quickly found their drivers licenses and noted their names and addresses. He tossed back the wallets toward the two fearful men, who looked confused.

"I know your names," said Daniel. "I know your addresses. If I catch you two bothering any Asian women ever again, I'll come after you. Is that understood?"

The two men looked at each other confused and nodded their heads vigorously when Daniel stammered, "Understood?!"

Daniel stood up and walked backwards and yelled, "Get out of here, and don't come back to these parts."

The driver pushed himself off his friend as he rubbed his throbbing chest. The other man clumsily climbed back into the passenger seat. Soon, the navy-blue car and the two miscreants drove away.

Daniel looked about with satisfaction and noted with surprise that no one else saw the incident. He quickly made his way back home the same way he came.

"Daniel?!" said his mother as she entered the door. She slipped out of her flats as she balanced a bag of groceries in her left arm. With her right hand, she lifted off her purse and dropped it and her keys onto the entry table.

"Daniel!" she said once more when suddenly, she felt the bag of groceries being lifted out of her left arm. Her brown eyes suddenly landed on Daniel who was smiling back at her.

"Daniel," she said with a smile. "There you are."

"Hi *mẹ*!" said Daniel as he looked into the bag of groceries as he saw the fresh baguette. "*Bánh mì?*"

His mother let out a sigh as she pressed down her clothes as she responded. "Yes, for dinner. Okay? I'm tired and I…"

"*Banh mi* is great, *mẹ*! I'll help you make them," said Daniel as he walked into the kitchen followed by his curious mother.

"What's going on, Daniel?" asked his mother.

As Daniel placed the bag of groceries onto the table, he turned to his mother and asked, "What do you mean?"

"You've been working really hard on your Vietnamese lessons, asking a lot of questions about Vietnam, and now you want to help me make *banh mi*, which you haven't done in years," his mother said.

Daniel smiled as his dark brown hair fell across his forehead slightly as his brown eyes looked back at his mother. He simply said, "Being Vietnamese is great, *mẹ*."

His mother felt her heart warm as she let out a smile. With a nod she said, "You're a good Vietnamese boy."

Daniel proceeded to help his mom empty the grocery bag.

* * *

As Sung's eyes adjusted, his laptop screen came into view, and he could suddenly see the progress his friends had made on StarCraft while he was away. He looked at the time and saw that he had only been gone for about thirty minutes. In the chat box, he saw his friends asking where he was, and he leaned back into his chair. After a few moments, he leaned in and pulled his keyboard forward.

"Hey guys, need to sign off. BBL," he typed into the chat box. Before his friends could respond, he signed off from StarCraft, leaving his friends to battle the Zerg.

Sung looked down at the Portal Book and saw his Korean name and he smiled.

"Kim Sung," he whispered as his Korean pride was stoked.

He gently closed it and stood up, pausing for a moment. He eased himself out from the tight corner that served as his study and gaming area. He picked up his phone from the nightstand and left his room.

He could smell something amazing coming from the kitchen, and he knew his mother was probably cooking up another delicious dinner for that Friday night. As he entered the kitchen, the scene of his mother bringing dishes to the dinner table confirmed his suspicions.

"*Eomma*," said Sung with a smile.

His mother, a slightly pudgy Korean woman with shoulder length hair and a jovial expression, looked up with a smile. "Sung, dinner is almost ready. Why don't you get your *appa*."

"Sure, where's…" said Sung as the sound of an electric saw drowned out his question. As the whirring of the circular blade cut through the air, Sung smiled and headed out the back door.

Directly outside in the backyard, Sung's father was bent over a workbench cutting boards from a plank of wood. There were about seven pieces of freshly cut breaking boards on the ground for the Tae Kwan Do classes that he taught. As he set aside the circular saw on the workbench, Sung appeared and bent down to pick up the boards.

"Sung," said his father. "What are you doing here? Shouldn't you be playing your game?"

Sung shrugged as he neatly stacked the boards into his hands and rose. He looked at his father and simply said, "*Appa*, what do you think about me going back to practice Tae Kwan Do with you?"

His father scoffed gently at him as he took the breaking boards from Sung. He stacked them on top of another set of breaking boards that he had cut earlier. "Sung, you gave that up a long time ago. It would be too much work to retrain you."

"*Appa*," said Sung. "I've been practicing, and I think I can teach…"

Sung's father let out a laugh and dismissed his son gently. "Sung, you're not ready to teach. You're not even ready to be a student."

"*Appa*," Sung respectfully pleaded. "Give me a chance."

Sung's father looked at him sternly and exhaled. He picked out two breaking boards, walked away and turned toward Sung. He held one board up and simply said, "Snap kick!"

To his father's utter surprise, the board in his hand cracked in two before he could even blink. He looked at the small piece of wood left in his hand and looked back up at Sung. He raised the other board in his hand, braced himself and yelled, "Spinning back…"

The snap took him by surprise as the speed of his son's heel sailed past him. He looked befuddled that the two boards had been so easily snapped with such precise kicks. Sung's father didn't say a word as he bolted back toward the workbench, picked up two more boards and spun around. He held one board and yelled out, "Jumping spinning kick!"

Sung flew and spun through the air with his heel out, easily snapping the board in two as his father brought up the second board as high as his arm could reach. "Other foot, reverse spin kick."

Sung planted his right foot down, spun counterclockwise as his left foot snapped into the board, shattering it.

As Sung resumed a ready stance, his father looked at his son in awe. "You've been practicing?"

Sung relaxed his hands and stance and sheepishly said, "Yah, I have, *appa*."

A smile erupted across his father's face just as his wife yelled from the backdoor, "*Aigo*! Stop the kicking and come in for dinner!"

Sung's father laughed as he and Sung bent down to pick up the broken pieces of the breaking boards. His father looked up at him and said, "You owe me four boards."

Sung smiled back and said, "Sure thing, *appa*."

* * *

The bright light faded away, and as soon as Yuka could discern that she was back by her bed, she quickly looked around and saw no one. All was quiet as she looked at the other empty beds nearby. She let out a sigh and thought it was as if nothing had happened while she was gone. She picked her up brush, dipped it into the ink, and started to manifest. It was the only thing that kept her happy and preoccupied while she was at a camp she didn't want to be in.

* * *

The warm glow of the light dissipated, and Clara looked back down at her green jade bracelet. She smiled, glad to have it back. As she sat in the chair, she heard the apartment door open and shut and some murmuring from outside her bedroom door. She got up and placed the Portal Book back into the center drawer of her desk. She turned and stared at her stuffed panda and said, "Have I got a story for you!"

Clara left her bedroom and walked down the hall, where her parents were talking. But her furtive footsteps weren't enough to hide her presence, and her father turned to her and said, "Hey, empress."

Clara couldn't help but smile. "Hey Baba, how was work?"

As her father started to bring over the dishes of food from the counter to the kitchen table, he replied, "Just glad it's Friday. Maybe after dinner and your lesson, we can watch a movie?"

"Sure Baba," said Clara as she went over to her mother. She admired her mother's profile, with her slim jawline and slightly wavy shoulder-length hair, which swayed a bit. As she picked up the last empty rice bowl to scoop rice into it from the rice cooker, her mother's jade bracelet caught her attention.

Clara looked at it with curious eyes as she grabbed the two rice bowls filled with rice. Her mother glanced down and without stopping her work, said, "Thank you, Clara."

"Mom?" asked Clara as she held onto the bowls as her mother finished filling the last one.

"Mmmm?" her mom mumbled as she closed the lid of the rice cooker.

"You got your jade bracelet from Po Po, right?"

"Yes," said her mother as she looked at Clara's curious eyes.

"And did Po Po get one from her mother? My great-grandmother?"

"I think so," said her mother as she nudged Clara to the dinner table.

Clara walked to her seat and placed a rice bowl in front of her father, who had just settled into his seat.

"What can you tell me about her?" asked Clara as she settled down into her seat.

Her mother sat down and placed her own rice bowl down in front of her and replied, "Well, I know she was a dress maker."

Clara's eyes lit up as she uttered, "A Qipao dressmaker?"

Clara's mother turned to her daughter, stared and asked curiously, "Yes, but how do you know that?"

Clara froze as the vision of her great-grandmother from the Jade Labyrinth in a Qipao appeared in her mind. She paused as her father also looked up curiously at her. She quickly recomposed herself and replied, "Well, what other dresses would they be making in China at that time?"

Her father looked at Clara's mother and nodded. "She's got a point."

"Huh," said her mother suspiciously as she picked up her chopsticks. "I guess so. So yes, your great-grandmother, my grandmother, made the most beautiful Qipaos."

Clara suddenly felt giddy and asked, "Can you tell me more about her? And my other great-grandparents?"

Her mother smiled and replied, "Let's eat first, okay?"

Clara smiled and picked up her chopsticks as she said to her father, "You too, Baba, can you tell me about your grandparents?"

Her father gulped down a bite of food as he replied, "Sure thing, empress."

TWENTY - NINE

Each heavy footstep landed on the dark stone with a low thud. The Warlock walked deliberately, taking his time as he entered his cavernous throne room. He saw before him his loyal Demon Lords of Nadi.

The Ox Head Demon Lord stood rigid on his spot, at attention as he watched his master walk by him. The Ox Head's muscular human-like frame was intimidating, clad in a leather outfit augmented with metal buttons and clasps. He held his trident proudly.

Next to him was the nine-tailed fox, who seemed to float above the spot she occupied. The folds of her flowing white robe shimmered ever so slightly each time she moved, her dark voluminous black hair contrasting against it. Her perfect angelic features belied her cunning intent. Her flared-out furry tails amplified her wondrous but deadly presence.

The third demon lord was an *oni*, an ogre-like creature. His muscles snarled over his frame and unlike the others, he was wearing loosely fitted clothing on the verge of falling off. There was more of a wild presence about him as his contorted brutish face looked as if he had been in too many battles.

Lastly, The Horse Head Demon Lord, the partner to the Ox Head, also stood rigidly on his spot. He too had a muscular human-like body and donned a similar dark leathery outfit. He looked ahead as he gripped his spiked club.

The Warlock slowly passed them, his presence by far dwarfing the others in the throne room. He turned to them and grunted as they looked ahead reverently. He resumed his walk up to his elevated bare stone throne. His battle armor, a mix of leather and metal, moved with every step of his grayish and brownish leathery skin. He turned from the throne and settled himself slowly into it, letting out a heavy sigh.

He eyed his loyal Demon Lords from left to right and took notice of the empty fifth spot. His gaze landed on the dark, glassy orb balanced on the right armrest. He placed his palm onto it, and soon it glowed gently as green swirls flowed within it. He let out another sigh.

He fingered the orb, delighting in the green glow emitted with each touch. His eyes shifted up toward the glass ceiling as he looked at the moons overhead. His eyes cast down onto his Demon Lords, and he spoke in a low rumbling voice.

"This new crop of warriors is very different than the ones before. They are more unpredictable and brash. That is good, as their inexperience has shown us many new things in this new cycle," said the Warlock as he let his last word linger in the air.

"The jade can be destroyed, rendering their battle armor useless, but it can also be replaced, it seems. The pandas were at full force in this second battle. And you—" he nodded towards the nine-tailed fox, "—you finally had another taste of siphoning the Qi from one of the young warriors who forgot his jade weapon. How foolish of him! But somehow, he was brought back to life. We were so close to rendering two kingdom armies useless. The third moon will be in alignment soon, let's see what your *onis* can do," said the Warlock as he looked dead straight at the *Oni* Demon Lord.

The mangled ogre-like creature nodded as did all the other Demon Lords. The Warlock's eyes shifted to his right and onto a stone circle, with five empty stone tablets on pedestals.

In a low rumbling voice that reverberated throughout the throne room, he declared, "I shall have the Portal Books!"

THANK YOU

If you have come to the end of "Clara Wu and the Jade Labyrinth," which is Book Two of the Clara Wu Books Series, I hope you enjoyed all the twists and turns and were inspired by the exploits of Clara Wu, Sung Kim, Yuka Satoh and Daniel Nguyen!

I also hope that you could identify with one or more of the characters. And let's not forget the Guardian Panda, White Tiger, Red Crown Crane and the Water Buffalo.

My goal is to create authentic Asian American stories so that Asian American readers can see themselves as the heroes. We've always been, we just need more writers to put them on paper.

Please tell your friends about this book series and flip to the section where I give some tips on how to promote this book to better Asian Representation!

A big thank you to SantiSann who refreshed the cover art to Book Two. Isn't it amazing? Check out SantiSann's work at:

Instagram: @santisann88

Another thank you goes out to Gloria Tsai for voicing the audio teaser for Book One which you may find on YouTube by searching for "Clara Wu." Check out her work at:

http://www.gloriatsai.com/voiceover.html

I also wanted to take a moment to thank my editor, Felicia Lee of Cambridge Editors, who has been my editor since my first book. Check out her profile at:

https://cambridgeeditors.com/editors/

Please be sure to check out **www.clarawubooks.com** and **www.vincentsstories.com** where you can check out my two other books, which are also available on Amazon:

The Purple Heart
The Tamago Stories

Continue your epic Asian American fantasy with book three: Clara Wu and the Rescue!

C3E4

"Clara Wu and the Portal Book," Book One of the Clara Wu Books, is now an Award-Winning Book! In the Fall of 2022, Clara Wu and her Guardian Panda showed fantasy fans that stories about Asian American heroes and their cultural animals can enrich the fantasy genre!

BOOK THREE

CLARA WU

AND THE

RESCUE

BY VINCENT YEE

AVAILABLE NOW!

ABOUT THE AUTHOR

Vincent Yee was born in Boston, Massachusetts. For most of his career, he has worked for several Fortune 100 companies in various managerial roles. At all other times, he has a vision…

"To write for better Asian Representation."

In 2022, he became an award-winning author for the first book in his YA-Fantasy series, "Clara Wu and the Portal Book," that placed second in the overall YA-Fantasy category at The BookFest. The remaining books of the "Clara Wu and the World of Azen," were all published in one year and they were: The Jade Labyrinth, Rescue, Final Battle and Warlock.

He has two other books prior and his first novel, "The Purple Heart," is a story about love and courage set during the Japanese American experience in WWII. His second book is a collection of 8 riveting contemporary Asian American short stories.

Vincent Yee was a former National President for the National Association of Asian American Professionals (NAAAP). He also co-founded the ERG at his last employer and led it with an amazing team, to be one of the largest ERGs with over 450+ members within a few months. He's also been known to create artistic culinary dishes for friends. When he is not writing, he may be binging a K-Drama on Netflix. He now lives in Cambridge, Massachusetts.

HOW TO SUPPORT

w w w . c l a r a w u b o o k s . c o m

Nothing makes a book popular and successful without its fans so please spread the word!

1) **FACEBOOK**
   Go to facebook.com/clarawubooks and **LIKE** the page.
2) **INSTAGRAM and TIK TOK**
   Go to Instagram and Tik Tok and like @clarawubooks
3) **SELFIE or PICTURE**
   TAKE a selfie/picture with yourself or your young reader that you are comfortable with, along with the book, and post to your social media and use the tags below.

   For Facebook and IG/Tik Tok tag @clarawubooks and use the hashtags #clarawubooks #AsianRepresentation #AsianStories #asianbookstagrammer

4) **WEB**
   Go to www.clarawubooks.com to find out the fun ways on how to engage with these books. You'll find my contact info there.
5) **AMAZON/GOODREADS**
   Please write a review for each book in the Clara Wu Books that you have read on Amazon or Goodreads.

6) **ASIAN SCHOOL**
   Spread the word at your child's weekend Asian programs (e.g. Chinese, Korean, Japanese, Vietnamese, etc), or martial arts/music/dance schools.

7) If you belong to a book club, please consider recommending this book for your next read. I will attend your book club over Zoom if so desired.

8) **EDUCATORS**
   Are you an elementary or high school teacher? This would be great for your students!

9) **LIBRARIES/BOOKSTORES**
   Talk to your library about adding this series to their collection. Over ten libraries in the greater Boston area now carry it.

10) **COMMUNITY ORGANATION/ERG**
   If you are part of any Asian American community organization or ERG/BRG/Affinity group, I'd be more than happy to be a speaker. Go to www.clarawubooks.com for more info.

11) If you know of any Asian American Influencers/Podcasters, please consider recommending this book to them.

12) If you would like to host a Meet the Author event over Zoom for your group of friends, your organization or your work AA group, I'll be there!

13) Lastly, you can **"Read It, Wear It!"** Flip to the next page to see the exciting **MERCH** items for Clara Wu and the World of Azen.

Let's **PROVE** that there is a market for positive and authentic Asian American stories especially ones that will give the next generation of Asian American readers, heroes that look like them.

READ IT
WEAR IT

clarawubooks.myshopify.com

Wear exciting merchandise featuring your favorite characters from the Clara Wu Books! Choose from over 100 items! Show your friends what an amazing fantasy story they've been missing! Another great way to spread the word!

DICTIONARY

Word	Language	Meaning	First Appeared In
abeoji	Korean	father	B1
aigo	Korean	oh my goodness – usually used to express annoyance or surprise	B2
Annyeonghaseyo	Korean	Hello	B2
Ao Dai	Vietnamese	A traditional Vietnamese dress that is a long gown worn with trousers.	B1
appa	Kokrean	Father informal, affectionate	B2
baba	Cantonese – Chinese	Father informal, affectionate	B1
bakemono	Japanese	A shape shifter that usually comes in the form of a beautiful woman to seduce unsuspecting men	B2
ban chans	Korean	A collection of side dishes like kimchi, radish or cucumber usually served along with meals.	B1
bánh mì	Vietnamese	A Vietnamese sandwich which may contain marinaded meat and fresh picked vegetables served in a soft baguette	B2
baos	Chinese	A Chinese white bun filled a variety of ingredients.	B1
budi	Korean	Please	B2
Bukdaemun	Korean	North Big Gate – One of the eight gates in Korea.	B1
cảm ơn bạn	Vietnamese	thank you	B1
chigae	Korean	Korean stew made from a variety of ingredients.	B1
chu	Cantonese	pillar	B2
dahm	Korean	wall	B1
dali	Korean	bridge	B1
đẩy	Vietnamese	thrust	B1
dò-jeh	Cantonese – Chinese	thank you	B1
dolgyuk	Korean	charge!	B2
domo arigato	Japanese	*Thank you very much*	B1
Dongdaemun	Korean	East Big Gate – One of the	B1

		eight gates in Korea.	
eomma	Korean	Mother informal, affectionate	B1
galbi	Korean	grilled ribs (aka kalbi)	B1
gam-sa-ham-ni-da	Korean	thank you	B1
gimbap	Korean	A roll of rice and cooked items wrapped in seaweed	B2
gong gyuck	Korean	attack	B1
gumiho	Korean	A version of the 9 tailed fox creature that is common in east Asian culture (aka kumiho)	B2
Hạ Long Bay	Vietnamese	Famous beautiful bay in Vietnam that is also a UNESCO World Heritage Site	B1
Hangul	Korean	Writing system of the Korean language.	B1
Huli jing	Chinese	A version of the 9 tailed fox creature that is common in east Asian culture	B2
Huo Dou	Chinese	A large black dog that can emit flames from its mouth.	B1
jinju	Korean	pearl	B1
jo sun	Cantonese – Chinese	Good morning in Cantonese	B1
joh-eun achim	Korean	*Good morning with beautiful sun*	B1
Jook	Cantonese	Similar to rice porridge served with slices of meat, preserved duck egg along with Chinese fried dough	B2
jōshō suru	Japanese	ascend	B1
kabe	Japanese	wall	B1
Kalbi	Korean	grilled ribs (aka galbi)	B2
Karate	Japanese	A Japanese martial art that means *empty hand*.	B1
kata	Japanese	In Karate, a set pattern of movements that is practiced as part of training.	B1
katana	Japanese	Usually refers to a long single edged sword usually used by the Samurai.	B1
kimchi	Korean	A spicy fermented cabbage that is a delicacy in Korea.	B1
kimono	Japanese	A beautiful and traditionally wrapped garment for	B1

		Japanese women that may come in a variety of colors and patterns.	
Konbanwa	Japanese	Good evening	B2
Kting voar	Vietnamese	Mystical horned creature that existed in Vietnam and Cambodia. Its true origin has never been determined though its unusual horns have left researchers puzzled about the creature.	B1
Kung Fu	Chinese	A Chinese martial art with many styles.	B1
makimono	Japanese	A Japanese roll of seaweed and sushi rice that may contain vegetables, fish or both.	B1
mẹ	Vietnamese	mother	B1
moushi wake arimasen deshita	Japanese	*No excuses can justify my actions and I apologize*	B1
Namdaemun	Korean	South Big Gate – One of the eight gates in Korea.	B1
ngọc trai	Vietnamese	pearl	B1
Ni Hao	Mandarin	Hello	B2
nigiri	Japanese	Usually, a ball of sushi rice that is topped off with raw fish or other seafood.	B1
nue	Chinese	A creature with the face of a monkey, a body of a tiger and a venomous snake as its tail	B2
ohayo gozaimasu	Japanese	good morning	B1
oni	Japanese	Ogre like creature that exists in Japanese folklore	B2
origami	Japanese	The art of folding paper.	B1
otosan	Japanese	father formal	B1
pãru	Japanese	pearl	B1
pho	Vietnamese	A Vietnamese soup noodle dish usually made from a slow cooked beef bone broth, with rice noodles and beef slices or brisket.	B1
Seodaemun	Korean	West Big Gate – One of the eight gates in Korea.	B1
seoping	Korean	surf	B1
Seosomun	Korean	West Small Gate - – One of the eight gates in Korea.	B1

shuriken	Japanese	Throwing star made popular in the era of Ninjas.	B1
Soohorang	Korean	Tiger of Protection – *Soohoo* means protection and *rang* comes from Ho-rang-i for tiger. Known to be a sacred guardian animal in Korea.	B1
Sungeuni mangeukhaeumnida	Korean	*Your grace is immeasurable*	B1
sừng	Vietnamese	horn	B2
Tae Kwan Do	Korean	A Korean martial art that is known for its powerful and dynamic kicks.	B1
taegeuk	Korean	In Tae Kwan Do, a set pattern of movements that is practiced as part of training.	B1
tamago	Japanese	Elegant Japanese version of an egg omelette	B2
tatami	Japanese	A type of traditional Japanese flooring.	B1
tei hum	Cantonese – Chinese	sinkhole	B1
teng-bing	Cantonese – Chinese	wall	B1
the-oung	Vietnamese	wall	B1
thit bo voi bo	Vietnamese	well known beef dish	B1
thù lao	Vietnamese	charge!	B2
tō	Japanese	Japanese pagoda like tower structure.	B1
tobu	Japanese	fly	B1
Vovinam	Vietnamese	A Vietnamese martial art	B1
yakitori	Japanese	skewered grilled meat	B1
yi ge jiu cai san xian jiao zi	Mandarin	One leek and bamboo dumpling	B2
yi ge bai cai san xian jiao zi	Mandarin	One cabbage and bamboo dumpling	B2
yi ge san xian jiao zi	Mandarin	One pea, carrot and bamboo dumpling	B2
Yonggirang	Korean	Tiger of Courage – *Yong-gi* for courage and *rang* comes from Ho-rang-i for tiger. The Guardian Animal from the White Tiger Kingdom.	B1
zao shang hao	Mandarin	good morning in Mandarin	B1
zhēnzhū	Mandarin	pearl	B1